A KNIGHT TO REMEMBER

AN ELISADE NOVEL

CEILLIE SIMKISS

CONTENTS

A KNIGHT TO REMEMBER

MASTER CORMAC LAMBERT, BLACKSMITH

ou could say that I had been having a fairly normal day. A knight had commissioned a new coif, my apprentice was whining about making nails, and I intended to spend the afternoon flirting with my friend the tailor whenever said apprentice was distracted by his character building assignment.

Normal, that is, until a muscular woman who looked resplendent in a deep violet riding gown walked into the smithy. She plunked down a cloth purse that was so heavy it barely jingled when it hit the top of the granite countertop that separated the storefront from the rest of the workshop. I looked up from the account books I was working on and she spoke as soon as she had my attention.

"I have a challenge for you, smith."

Her voice was bright and steady, much like the smile that played across her golden brown face. She had a lilting accent that reminded me of home. I closed the book I was working on and placed my pen back into its holder, turning on my best salesman grin. It was clear from this woman's clothing that she had money.

"Cormac Lambert at your service. How can I help you, my lady? A new suit of mail for your betrothed? A new sword for your father or brother?"

The forge behind him had gone suspiciously quiet. He glanced back and saw that his apprentice was staring slack jawed at the noble visitor, who stood with her back ramrod straight before him.

"Or perhaps you would like to hire my useless apprentice?" I growled. The impudent boy grinned at me before going back to his work.

"As tempting as that sounds, I have a proposition that I think you will find much more interesting," she informed me. Her glinting hazel eyes never left my face. I raised an eyebrow at her and gestured to the stool that I knew stood in front of her on the other side of the counter.

"Interesting, eh? Let's talk then."

SER GENEVIEVE OF TEAGAN, KNIGHT OF ELISADE

As I took my seat at the counter, the smith asked his apprentice to finish up his batch of nails and then bring out refreshments. We both watched quietly as he hammered each strip on all four sides to create a point, then sliced off the nail to make sure each was the right length with a practiced hand. He hung his apron on the wall once he was finished and bowed to us both before scurrying out of the room. He looked to be a few years younger than I was, maybe fifteen or sixteen. Soot marked the tanned skin where he'd likely wiped sweat from his eyes with the back of his hands, and his eyes were the deep brown of healthy forest loam. With his easy smile and skills, I knew he would be a handsome man in a few years' time.

"He doesn't seem so useless to me," I told Cormac. "At least when it comes to nails."

He laughed so loudly and deeply that it was almost as if someone had struck a gong in the smithy.

"Oh, he isn't. He's one of the better apprentices I've had, and he knows it. I've learned that you can't tell them that all the time, though. It goes to their heads and soon enough they're so full of hot air they can't come into the smithy because their mouths act as a bellows whenever they open them."

That startled a laugh out of me, just in time for the boy to come back in with a carefully balanced tray that held two cups, a bottle of fruit juice and a pitcher of water. I could feel Cormac's eyes on me as I thanked him for the refreshments, and guessed that he was trying to figure out who I was. After a sip, I decided to give him a hint.

"What's your name, son?"

The boy bowed before smiling back up at me and answering.

"Finn, my lady."

"Don't let your old master here get you down, Finn," I said with a wink. "You made those nails more skillfully than many of the knights in the palace ever managed. You're probably even better at it than I am, even though I trained under Cormac here when I was just a wee thing."

Finn blushed and started to answer but was interrupted when the smith jumped from his stool in surprise. I grinned at him, clapping my hands together lightly in delight. He walked around the counter to greet me properly with the bow and a handshake. His palms were rough even against my own callused one.

"Lady Genevieve of Teagan, as I live and breathe! I've been trying to figure out who you were since you walked in! "

"In the flesh! Though you should know it's actually *Ser* Genevieve now."

"You were officially knighted! Congratulations, ser! I was so used to seeing you in those grubby trousers you used to run in and out of my Teagan smithy in that I didn't recognize you in all of this." He gestured to the outfit I wore, which was admittedly significantly nicer than what Mother had allowed me to run around in before I'd become a page.

"Yes, I was knighted last fall. It's good to see you too, Cormac. I won't even be offended that you didn't recognize me at first, though I am technically still wearing trousers. "

He looked at where I sat on the stool, confused.

I spread my legs ever so slightly to show off the fact that there was a split in the skirt that made it into a pair of pants. It was one of my favorite modifications to make to my fashionable clothes. The rest of the time, I just wore trousers.

"I should have known. You never would ride in a dress if you could help it. I'm glad to see you haven't changed much."

I winked at him before pouring myself a glass of fruit juice.

"Would you like some?"

He shook his head, pouring water into the other cup on the tray and returning to his own stool.

"Now that you've remembered who I am, shall we get down to business?"

"Absolutely, but first, let me take care of something."

He spun on his stool to face his apprentice. Finn had been tidying the workshop while we talked.

"Finn, it's about time for you to take a lunch break. Come back when the bell strikes three and we can finish tidying up together."

The boy bowed to his master, grabbed a satchel from behind the counter and scampered off. As soon as the door swung shut behind him, I fixed my gaze on the smith. He hadn't changed much in the years since I'd seen him. His hair was in the same messy ponytail and he had the same scraggly beard I remembered, though his face was more wrinkled now.

"Now, how busy are you? I have a challenge that could make your business famous around the world."

He cocked a greying eyebrow at me and I grinned.

"Famous, eh? What have you got for me, Ser? I can hear you out at the very least, and maybe point you in another direction if it's not something I can handle."

I folded my hands in my lap, running the thumb of one hand over the knuckles of the other. I took a deep breath, trying to contain my excitement and nervousness about what I was about to ask him to do.

"I need a dress for the king's ball in November, and I want you to make it."

Nearly a minute passed where we both just stared at each other. Cormac's jaw was nearly on the floor. I knew it was probably the strangest request he had ever received.

"Ser, you realize this is a blacksmith's forge, and not a tailor's shop, right? I do not have the skills to make a dress. I make chain mail and ornamental ironwork, I'm not a dressmaker."

"Ah, but that's where you're wrong. I think that, with some adjustments, you could make a stunning chain mail dress, with some ornamental pieces."

The blacksmith studied my face, his curiosity plain in the focus of his gaze and tilt of his head.

"Okay, I'll bite. Give me some more information."

I had to stop myself from squealing with glee. A smile spread across my face as I dove into the satchel I had brought with me, digging through it until I found the small, bound notebook I was searching for.

"I've got a basic sketch here. The rules are that you have to be able to fight, so it can't be too tight, but it also can't be too frilly. I know that plate mail won't allow me to dance, but if you know of a tailor that might work with us, I'm sure that they could help with the logistics of how it could work with mail."

I knew I was babbling, but I needed to get it all out before he made up his mind. Without saying anything, he gestured for the book and I handed it to him.

"I know it isn't done in quite the latest style, but it's flattering to my thick muscles in a way that I love, and allows me freedom of movement that I'll need as part of the honor guard."

He studied it for several moments, tapping a callused finger on the paper in thought before clearing his throat.

"I have a tailor friend not far from here. How about we take a wander over there and let them have a look and see if it's possible?"

This time I didn't even try to hold back the squeal of joy. Jumping up from the stool, I nearly toppling over when one leg of my pants got caught on my other foot. Catching myself on the countertop, I flushed hotly in embarrassment.

"Now, see, if you'd done that when you walked into my shop, I would've known exactly who you were," Cormac laughed. I couldn't help but laugh with him. He was right.

He held out a hand to steady me as I got my wardrobe malfunction in order, then handed my sketchbook back to me.

"Come along, lass. It's a short walk from here. Let me close up and leave a note for Finn in case he comes back early, and we can walk over."

MX. POPPY OF ELISADE, TAILOR

The sea breeze swirled into my shop through the dark green shutters, twisting the fabrics that dressed the mannequins before finding their way out the cut out windows of the arched doorway and back into the streets of Elisade.

It was a nice way to alleviate the heat that came from the number of people moving around. The morning had been busy, thanks to the announcement of the impending ball. It would be the highlight of the spring season or I'd eat the jaunty cap that kept my long curls out of my face.

Just as the shop began to clear out, something else came in through the window - a deep, booming voice that I recognized immediately.

"Hullo! May we come in?"

We? Crossing the room to look out the window, I was surprised to see that Cormac was accompanied by a well-dressed young woman who was nearly as tall as he was.

I didn't recognize her, but judging by her muscles, exquisite clothing, and gait, she had to be a knight. She stopped short in the doorway, her eyes wide as she looked around.

My chest swelled a little bit with pride as I looked at it as she might. The shelves Cormac had helped me build last year reached the ceiling and were packed with bolts of fabric organized by color then by the type of fabric within that. Just the way it needed to be in order to find the perfect fabric to complement an outfit.

"Welcome, welcome! I'm Poppy, the nonbinary proprietor here. Are you a friend of Cormac's? It's a pleasure to meet you!"

I shook her hand and pressed a friendly kiss to Cormac's cheek.

"Thank you, Poppy! I'm Ser Genevieve of Teagan, and Cormac and I go a long ways back. Your shop is absolutely lovely," Genevieve said. Her face was still full of wonder as she looked around.

"Why thank you! I designed it myself. I had this shop built from the ground up to my specifications nearly a decade ago, and it has served me well ever since."

"Poppy was one of the first people I met here in the city when I left Teagan. Their work is beautiful and they have the best selection of fabrics in the city," Cormac bragged.

I tried not to blush. Failing that, I tried to distract them from it by pouting playfully at Cormac.

"And yet he still won't let me make him anything pretty!"

Cormac started blushing as he waved a hand at me dismissively.

"What use is pretty for a blacksmith? Everything I own has singe marks on it. There's no use in my having pretty clothes. Besides, we aren't here for me, Poppy."

"Of course you aren't," I sighed. Planting my hands on my hips, I turned back to the knight. "Ser Genevieve of Teagan, how may I assist you today?"

The woman ducked her head shyly. Cormac nudged her, and she began digging through her leather satchel. I took advantage of the time to look more closely at her outfit. Whoever had created it had done it well. Nearly as well as I would have. I would have made sure it had deeper pockets, though.

She produced a small leather-bound book that looked like a sketchbook. Without speaking, she opened it and handed it to me.

I felt my jaw drop in shock as I looked over the sketch. A long-sleeved gown with what looked like a leather and chainmail bodice had been drawn, rather skillfully, on the page she showed me. Below the bodice, cloth and chainmail had been layered like the petals of a rose to create a skirt that would be beautiful and protective.

"What on earth do you need a chainmail dress for?"

That seemed to be the key to untying Genevieve's tongue. She opened her mouth to speak, but I realized its purpose.

"Wait, I know. You're one of the honor guards for the Midwinter Ball, aren't you?"

She beamed at me.

"Yes, and it's such an honor since I was just knighted last fall! But, my mother was planning to have me meet a suitor, and I desperately don't want to meet someone for the first time in plate mail. I love my knight work, but I just... I want to be pretty when I make my debut as a marriageable knight. Is that weird?"

I laughed.

"Not at all, sweetheart. Let me figure this out. I see why you brought Cormac along, though." I turned my attention to him. "Do you think this is possible, old friend?"

"I think it is, if we can find a fabric that is both to Ser Genevieve's tastes and can hold up my lightest chainmail."

I ran my fingers over the sketch, thinking out loud.

"What if we made the dress two separate pieces, connected by the chainmail around her middle, and... maybe a sheer fabric over the top here?"

Cormac chewed the inside of his bottom lip in thought while his eyes followed my fingers on the sketch.

Genevieve spoke up, and we both turned to look at her.

"I would like it if it could accentuate my waist a little, like today's gown does, if that's possible. I worry that a sheer fabric for the top piece would make me look more like a shield than a shield maiden, if that makes sense?" Genevieve's thin brows were furrowed, but I just waved at her.

"Of course, of course. You want to accent your feminine charms, eh? We can do that. What about a mail corset piece, attached to pliable leather?"

I could see from the light in Genevieve's eyes that she liked that idea.

"I think we have a winner," Cormac laughed. "But what about the skirt? We want it to be heavy enough to defend her, but also not take out her dance partner's ankles at every turn."

I snapped my fingers at him, knowing exactly what I wanted. Gliding over to the rolling ladder that was attached to the shelves where the white, cream and tan fabrics were, I grinned at him. I climbed up nimbly, grateful again that Cormac had helped me install the shelves on each of the walls. It made it so much easier for me to get the fabrics from the top of the shelf.

Looking at the shelf, I realized I needed more information to choose a fabric.

"Genevieve, my girl, what are your house colors? I know that Teagan has a blue base, but I cannot remember the others."

"Cream, blue and black," she listed automatically. "We don't have to have our coat of arms on anything, though if we wanted to work a leaf pattern into it anywhere, that would be lovely."

"What kind of leaf?" I asked, tapping a finger on my chin while I glanced through the fabrics. There were a lot of different types, after all, and I needed to make sure that the fabric would hold the embroidery well if it were a more complex look.

"Oh, oak, sorry."

A cool colored cream in a sturdy fabric, then.

"Oak leaves will not be a problem, particularly with this color scheme. Perhaps Cormac could use some copper in the mail and use it as a motif?"

"You are going to force me to get real creative, aren't you?" Cormac grumbled.

I grinned wolfishly at him.

"You know that I always aim to make people challenge themselves. Why should you be any different, old man?"

"You are two years older than me, Poppy," Cormac reminded me with a roll of his eyes. "You don't get to call me old."

"I do when you act like it! I don't think anyone has ever accused me of being an old soul."

He smiled at me wryly.

"That we have not. Now, can we get back to business? You're confusing Genevieve."

"Yes we can. Come and get these from me, please."

He maneuvered himself so that he was directly next to the ladder. I lowered two different bolts of fabric to him and began to descend the ladder.

Once my feet were firmly on the ground, I turned back to the knight. She was watching us with a soft smile on her face.

"I didn't know you two were together. Cormac, you should have told me this was your partner," she chided him gently.

His face turned as red as if he'd spent the full day working in the forge, and he tried to sputter out a reply. I just laughed.

"It may yet happen, but he hasn't quite caught me yet," I said with a wink at Cormac. His face got even redder and I smiled.

"I see." Genevieve raised an eyebrow at both of us. Cormac exchanged a hopeful glance with her, but didn't say anything before she cleared her throat.

"Now, do you two think that this is actually possible? Mama didn't think anyone would be able to do it."

Cormac looked at me, his face glowing with a fierceness that told me he wanted to take on this challenge. I crossed my arms, grinning at her.

"We absolutely do."

DUKE AVERY OF WOLVINGTON

A series of knocks startled me as I sat on a chaise lounge in the library, nearly causing me to drop the book I was holding. I blinked several times as I tried to focus my eyes on the world around me instead of the pages in my hands.

"You need to see a physician to get some spectacles," my mother's voice rang out through the open door, startling me again. I jumped, actually dropping my book this time. "Why on earth is it so dark in here, Avery?"

She lit the lamp next to the door and I grimaced at the brightness of the light.

"It wasn't dark when I started reading?" I offered in my defense. Sitting up, I adjusted my binder so it would stop cutting into my armpits. If these things weren't so useful, no one would ever wear them.

"That isn't an excuse, and you know it, young man." She placed her hands on her hips. Even though her face was in shadow, I knew she was glaring at me. We'd had this conversation about a thousand times over the course of my life.

"And yet it is my reason for it being dark in my library," I told her cheekily. "Now, did you actually want something, or did you just come in here to lecture me?"

She stepped forward and I saw her in all her glory.

She wore a simple gray poplin house dress that would have had a less striking person mistaken for one of the servants. Dowager Duchess Celeste of Wolvington was a stunning woman who got even more striking with every year that passed. She had always been tall and even after bearing several children, her waist was almost waspish. Like usual, her curly graying hair had been twined into a series of long, thin braids that were then twisted and pinned away from her dark brown face that was a few shades darker than my own bronzed one. Her brown eyes glinted in the lamplight as she looked at me across the room.

"We've received news from the capital. Your brother is throwing a ball in your nephew's honor and he's requested your presence at your earliest convenience."

My eyebrows shot up. That was certainly a surprise.

2

I could feel myself almost bouncing in joy in the saddle as I made my way back to my family's house in town. I could hardly believe that Cormac and Poppy were going to make the dress I'd dreamed up a real thing.

My mother had arrived in the capital last week for the beginning of the winter social season and my father would be coming in the next week or so with my siblings. I couldn't wait to see their faces when they saw the chainmail and silk masterpiece that I intended to wear as part of the honor guard.

The prince's ball was to be the last event of the social season, a move which I suspected was planned strategically for both political and social purposes. Each noble family was expected to have a representative at the ball.

I was in luck, because I knew that gown was going to take a lot of work for Cormac and his apprentice on the front end and a lot for Poppy and their apprentices once the chainmail was complete. It really was a challenge for everyone involved, myself included.

Mama had tested her full range of emotions, starting with delight and pride when I told her I'd been chosen as part of the honor guard and moving quickly to horror when she realized that meant that I would have to wear my parade plate mail.

I'd always known she had a flair for the dramatic, but I was pretty sure if we'd put her on a stage, the performance would have won awards.

"I've been planning to take you to your first ball and introduce you properly to all of the marriageable gentleman. How will I do that if you are wrapped up in plate mail?" she had wailed piteously.

I had had to hold back a snort of laughter that Mama would have declared horribly unladylike.

"Plate mail is well and good for battle and ceremonies," Duchess Vivienne had said crisply once she'd calmed down. "It can even look quite dashing. But it has no place on an honor guard in the best guarded city, in the palace of Elisade. What will you be able to do that the other guards will not?"

In my mother's defense, I had to admit that she had a point. The prince was in very little danger at a ball held in his own castle. The palace had been built and warded specifically to keep anywho wished ill on the royal family out of it.

But it did mean that things had been a little awkward when I'd reported for duty. I asked the other knights what they had worn as part of the honor guard, and they had looked at me as if I'd grown a second head. They had all simply worn their ceremonial plate armor and been done with it without a thought to whether their mother would be able to pair them up nicely with a dance partner or not.

I almost longed to not have to worry about getting married the way many of my fellow knights did, but at the same time, I wanted a partner even more. The Goddess knew I was tired of living alone in the town house when I was stationed in the capital, which had been most of the time for the year I'd been a knight.

And perhaps... perhaps it would even help me do what I hadn't managed yet - to catch the attention of the man I'd been crushing on ever since I first met him at my younger sister's graduation five years ago. Duke Avery of Wolvington.

Part of the problem I'd had was that I was a very different person from my younger sister. Where Alys was bright and cheerful and loved to be the center of attention at a party, I had always been more comfortable with the much simpler rules of etiquette on the dueling grounds and practice fields. I knew that I could fight with any weapon I put in my hand without a second thought, but I also knew that there were other conversational weapons that I was woefully unprepared to deal with.

The other part of the problem was that he was third in line for the throne after King Bayard's children, Prince Julian and Princess Cecelia. He was King Father Victor's oldest son from his second marriage, and I was a junior knight from the duchy next to his mother's.

Even if Duke Avery wasn't interested, perhaps I would be able to get Mama to introduce me to someone interesting. I knew most of the young noblemen and women in the country, thanks to serving alongside them or their siblings as a knight, but surely an event like this would draw some interesting foreign nobles.

Mama would know, and would be able to help me prepare for it, I thought. Much like her younger daughter, Duchess Vivienne was a skilled socialite. At the very least, I would have to get used to dancing in a dress again. Asking my mother for help might make the next two months a little bit more stressful, but I thought that it might be worth it to put some effort into a skill I needed.

Blinking, I realized that I could see our home. I had been so caught up in my thoughts that I hadn't even noticed where I was going.

My horse slowed to a canter and then to a halt at our stables. One of the stable hands waited inside the doorway, taking the reins from me. Swinging out of the saddle, I walked into the house with a mission. It was time to ask my mother for her help.

AVERY

My mother spent the entire trip talking to me about this and that noble whose daughter was looking for an arranged marriage, most of whom were significantly younger than me. Marriage for people of my stature was rarely a love match, but she had always promised me that I would have as much input on who I married as she had, especially since she wasn't worried about heirs. Since I would never be able to get anyone pregnant and had no interest in becoming pregnant, it was unlikely that I would ever have children of my own, which was fine by all of us. It did make a difference to the families of some of the other nobles, though, and my marriage prospects. Mother took that into consideration with all the matches she considered.

"We're almost there, son!"

Father, known to the rest of the world as King Father Victor of Elisade, called out from the front of the carriage. I could imagine the wide grin on his face that he always wore when he traveled. He had been riding up front with the driver for most of our travels. He said he loved to feel the open air on his face, and that might have been true, but I also knew that it helped with his motion sickness to sit up front.

Even though we had only been traveling for three days, I felt like I had lived an entire lifetime in the carriage by the time we spotted the outline of Elisade's capital city in the distance from the carriage window. The blue gray stone of the walls that encircled the city nearly blocked out the view of the ships that had docked at the largest naval port in the country.

I wondered how Father felt returning to the city again. He avoided the capital at all costs now that he was no longer in charge of the realm and I had taken over the majority of the ducal duties from Mother. The city where he and his first wife, Amelie, had ruled together was full of hard memories for him after her assassination many years ago, but I knew he wouldn't want to miss his eldest grandson's first ball, either. Even if said grandson was less than a decade younger than me.

Julian was a pretty cool kid now that we were grown, though I had often found him rather irritating on the summers he spent in Wolvington. I suppose that was normal when there were eight years difference between two children who were expected to spend time together when they had basically nothing in common other than family. Especially when one of them was always running around and getting into the other's schoolwork and experiments. Now we had enough common ground to stand on and could actually stand each other's' company for long enough to make it through a family dinner or an extended weekend visit. I was grateful for that since we would all be staying in the palace for this visit at Bayard's insistence. He had a habit of doing that, insisting on things that made the rest of us uncomfortable, which I supposed was not unusual for a king, but it was very annoying for a family member.

"Do we have any plans once we reach the palace?" I asked my mother, who was still looking out the window. She jumped as if she'd forgotten that I was there.

"Hm? Oh, no. I will be asking for a piping hot bath for myself and your father. Even though we've been in the carriage, I feel like I'm coated in road dust and I can't stand it."

I could certainly understand that feeling. A hot bath sounded perfect to work out the aches that spread through my lower back and legs. That would go a long way to making me feel more human than I did at the moment. It would also mean I'd have to put on my binder again and refresh the spells that helped me transition, which was less exciting, but made me feel better about the way I was presenting myself to the shark-infested waters that were the palace gossips. They could be vicious when they wanted to be, and a ball like this was sure to have them smelling blood. Mother turned back to me, an eyebrow raised.

"Why? Did you have something you wanted to do when we arrived?"

"Oh, no. Not at all. I just wanted to make sure there wasn't anywhere else we needed to be, what with Bayard's tendency to overschedule everyone."

Her eyes glinted with mirth. She knew well my preference for keeping my own company whenever possible, even when I was with family.

"We made sure to set the remainder of today and tomorrow to ourselves to recoup from the journey, aside from family dinners. After that, we're more or less at Bayard's mercy. I'll be sure to make your excuses if you find more pleasing companions to spend time with."

The carriage slowed to a halt. Peeking out the window, I realized that we were already at the city's gates. It was time for the spring season to begin with us as a part of it.

GENEVIEVE

I took my time walking into the house, looking around at the houses around me. They were nowhere near as sprawling or as decadently decorated as those that we nobles resided in on our estates, but they were hardly small, either.

All of them looked similar, which made sense since they were all builds of the same tan brick and dark slate roofs. The home that I had spent half of my life in always brought a smile to my face when I saw it.

My mother had always made sure that there was no chance of anyone mistaking it for another noble family's house from the exterior by decorating with cream and navy curtains in every room and hiring a craftsman to create a bronze leaf pattern on the outside of each window. The fence that marked our lawn off from the road had the same leaf pattern worked into the iron. I'd always found it beautiful and comforting, and today was no different.

The front door, which held a carving of the house crest, swung inward, revealing the butler who had been around since before I could remember.

"Welcome home, Ser Genevieve," Ernest called to me, his voice gravelly and kind behind his gruff exterior. As I got closer, I could see he was smiling underneath the dark beard that he kept cropped close to his pale face.

"Thank you, Ernest. I'm glad to be home. Is the Duchess home?"

"I believe you will find her in the master study. She has been dealing with the accounts all afternoon and could probably use the company... and perhaps a pot of tea?"

He winked a green eye at me and I grinned. The man must have been blessed by the goddess to always know what the family would need. Mama was always a grouch after dealing with the accounts all day. I couldn't blame her, given that accounts for a duchy of our size were an ordeal at the best of times.

I made my way to the kitchen where the staff was busy working on our late supper. It smelled of roast turkey and the yeast of dinner rolls. I couldn't wait to sit down and eat with everyone.

Eating alone had always been something I detested, so I avoided it whenever possible. Once I had taken up semi-permanent residence in the town house, I'd made it the household policy that any of the staff who wanted to sit down and eat together would be able to, whether I was home or not. It meant some things got delayed in the evenings, but it was worth it to spend time with the people of our household on a regular basis.

"Betsy, might I trouble you for a pot of tea for Mama?"

"Sure thing. Put together a tray and I'll have it sent up for you in a jiffy," the jovial older woman said, never turning to face me. She didn't need to. She knew all of our preferences almost better than we did, and I knew my way around the kitchen.

I pulled a wooden tray off of the shelf near the open doorway, setting it on the end of the solid slab of granite that served as the counter top.

Grabbing two ceramic mugs from the second shelf, I nestled them into the indentations that had been worn into the tray from years of use. According to etiquette, we should have been using teacups and saucers, but we didn't care about silly things like that when there was no one watching. I settled a porcelain teapot into the center of the tray and looked for the sachets of tea leaves I had prepared earlier in the week. Finding several, I nestled them into the bottom of the pot and waited.

Around me, the other workers ignored me, chopping vegetables and prepared the fruit for the evening's dessert - Mama's favorite apple charlotte, made with homegrown apples from the estate.

"Out of the way," Betsy called. I stepped away and she swooped in, filling the pot with boiling water and leaving a cloud of steam behind her. "Now, do you think you can manage take that up the stairs without spilling it, or should I send one of the maids up with you?"

I flushed, knowing that her question was a sincere one, and

that she had reason to ask. I had been very clumsy when I was younger, something that had only been cured by years of fighting practice. However, I also knew that if Mama saw me carrying my own tea tray, she'd have a fit.

"I would appreciate a maid's help," I told her. "The Duchess and I will be in the master study."

Betsy nodded and put the cauldron back over the fire.

"I'll have a maid up in just a moment. Now, if you'll excuse me, I have work to do, and your mother will want to talk to you."

She bustled away without another word, which is exactly what I needed to do. I made my way out of the kitchen, trying to figure out exactly how I would ask my mother for her help to flirt appropriately with a Duke.

I made my way up the stairs to the third floor, one hand lightly trailing the floral carved wooden banister as I went.

Because she and my father were no longer living in the house as often, they had insisted that I take the master suite instead of staying in my childhood bedroom on the second floor. The master suite was the only one equipped with a study of its own, which wasn't usually a problem.

When I reached the third floor landing, I paused to get the lay of the land. I couldn't hear my mother, but that wasn't surprising, since the study was still several rooms away.

Turning right into my bedroom, I tossed my satchel onto the table alongside the other letters and miscellaneous things I'd never managed to put away. A few pages scattered to the floor and I sighed. I really needed to deal with all of that. But it had waited this long without being dealt with. It would last another day or two as it was.

Slipping my shoes off, I padded over to the study door on the opposite side of the room. I could hear the fast rustling of papers and knew that Ernest had been right about Mama's mood.

I crossed my fingers, hoping that it hadn't been brought on by me messing something up. With my other hand, I knocked on the solid oak door. The sound echoed that of my anxious heartbeat in my ears.

The rustling stopped. I could almost imagine my mother blinking at the papers in front of her, trying to figure out where the sound had come from. I knocked again.

"Who is it?" She called out.

"Mama, it's me."

"Oh come in, dear! It's not locked."

Smiling, I opened the door to reveal my mother's hazel eyes squinting over the top of her thin glasses at me. Her face had deeper lines than I remembered, but she was still one of the prettiest women I'd ever met. Her golden brown skin was a few shades lighter than my own, since she took care to keep herself protected from the sun's harsh rays.

"I'd be more concerned if it was! This door only locks when Ernest activates the spell, remember?

She smiled crookedly at me.

"You know, I'd forgotten that somehow. Perhaps it's time to change that, since there are no longer troublesome children in the house."

She set her glasses down on top of the account books, then used both hands to rub her eyes.

"I would have thought it would be something we could have changed years ago, honestly."

"You know full well there's a reason there were never locks on any of these doors. Your sister was a hellion. Can you imagine if she had locked herself in here and burned all the account books instead of burning her own belongings?"

I shuddered at the thought of losing years of house records in one of Aly's tantrums when she was younger. At nineteen, she was now a pretty powerful witch. However, Alys had discovered her affinity for offensive magic at the tender age of seven.

At the time, her most important concerns were how to get the largest slice of cake from Betsy, how to avoid going to bed on time, and how to cause the most trouble for her pre-teenaged older sister, all of which had resulted in some unfortunate property damage before we had found a tutor who helped her to control it.

Mama fixed me with a stare that made me feel like she could see right through me, patting the overstuffed chair next to her.

"You didn't come in here to muse about your sister's childhood troubles and locks, I'm sure. What's going on, my dear?"

I sat, squirming in the chair from nerves and in an attempt to get comfortable.

"Actually, I came to ask you for some advice." I let my tone turn the statement into a question, giving her an out.

Her face lit up, her thin, painted lips turning up into a catlike grin. Of course she wouldn't take the out.

"Why, if I have any to offer, you are welcome to it! Tell Mama what the problem is."

"Well... it's a little bit delicate."

The duchess arched her eyebrows at me.

"Delicate, you say? I don't think you've ever had a delicate question for me. How delightful!"

Now I remembered why I never asked my mother for advice. Resisting the urge to roll my eyes, I took a deep breath and released it in a whoosh.

"Mama, don't make this weird. I'm already vulnerable here."

Laughing lightly, she turned her chair so that it faced mine. Crossing her legs at the ankle, she nodded at me expectantly.

"So, remember how you told me that you wanted to introduce me to all of the eligible nobles at the ball?"

She nodded, and opened her mouth to speak. I held up a finger and she closed her mouth again.

"Well, I got to thinking about it, and I wanted to ask your advice."

"Wait, but that was before I knew you were going to be part of the honor guard," she cut in. "I cannot introduce you properly if you're wearing full plate mail."

"Well, that's what I came to talk to you about. I spent the morning commissioning a gown."

Mama's posture straightened ever so slightly and her jaw dropped.

"What do you mean? Are you not going to be a part of the honor guard? Whyever not? It is an honor for you to be chosen so young!"

"No, no, let me explain, Mama. I spoke with Knight Commander Cedric about your concerns. They said that if I could get a gown that I was able to fight in with enough notice, that had at least a layer of chainmail, that they would approve it for wear at Prince Julian's ball."

Mama's eyes lit like the wick of a candle.

"Why, that's wonderful!" she exclaimed. "But how on Earth are you going to be able to wear a gown with a layer of chain mail in it? You won't be able to dance in a mail shirt. It would be scandalous, and hardly any prettier than plate mail."

"That's the thing!" I nearly shouted in excitement. I brought my voice back to a normal volume before continuing. "I found a blacksmith and tailor that already work together, and the blacksmith is going to specially design some chain mail to be worked into the gown. Here, let me show you the sketch."

I reached for my satchel, then remembered I'd tossed it on my desk.

"Just a moment. Oh!"

I opened the study door to find someone else standing there, surprising both myself and the servant carrying the tray of now-steeped tea.

They wore the simple black trousers and white shirt that all of the servants wore, with a mulberry scarf around their neck that contrasted well with their pale blonde hair, which was tied up into a loose bun.

"Oh, I'm sorry, Juniper!"

"I'm so sorry, miss!"

We spoke at the same time and then laughed together.

"Please come in. I just needed to fetch something," I told them. They did as they were told, setting the tray on the end of the desk and serving my mother while I fetched the sketchbook. Crossing the threshold to my own room, I dug into my satchel and pulled out my notebook. Dashing back into the study, Juniper was pouring my tea.

They placed the now full, steaming mug of tea on the end table next to my chair, and bowed.

"Is there anything else I can do for you, Your Grace?"

Mama smiled graciously but shook her head.

"No, this is more than enough, Juniper. Thank you. And tell your mother I said hello."

"I will, Your Grace. Thank you."

They blushed, smiling up at Mama as they left the room.

"I've got my sketch here. I made a copy of it for Poppy and Cormac, but here's the original."

"For whom?"

"Sorry, I got ahead of myself. The blacksmith and tailor. You'd remember Cormac from Teagan, Mama!"

"The blacksmith you apprenticed for, for a summer? I didn't realize he would be willing to take something like this on."

She looked over the sketch appraisingly.

"This is quite a lovely design, Genevieve. This might just work, even for Knight Commander Cedric's severe requirements. You can even add your pauldrons on top of the sleeves here, and make it even more knight-like."

"Oh, you're right. That's brilliant!"

"Otherwise, you designed this beautifully and chose an

excellent blacksmith. If this Poppy is as good as he is, then this gown will come together in no time."

I beamed at my mother.

"I'm so glad you approve. It will be pricy, but it will be worth it, I think. Now, onto the delicate part..."

Vivienne laughed.

"What can I help you with, my dear?"

"Well, it's about a man."

Vivienne threw back her head and laughed. The mid-afternoon sunlight glinted off of her white teeth.

"The most delicate things usually are."

I knew she was right about that.

"Well... going back to the introductions, I was wondering if you could introduce me to the Duke of Wolvington?"

I looked up at my mother through my eyelashes, biting my teeth

"The King's son? Duke Avery? That Duke of Wolvington?"

"Yeah. I think he's really handsome, and I know he's not seeing anybody? If I've got to be introduced to the entire kingdom, then I'd like to be introduced to him."

Mama waved a hand at her face dramatically, wiping fake tears from her eyes with the other.

"My baby's all grown up and asking me to introduce her to a man who is in line for the throne. I never thought this day would come."

"Mama, there is no need to be this dramatic. I've asked you to introduce me to people before!"

"Yes, but not the King's second son! Everyone you've asked me to introduce you to is someone you needed to know as a knight, not someone you thought was worth courting. This is a momentous occasion!"

I knew my face was bright red from embarrassment. I wanted

to hide, but knew that I wouldn't be able to until this conversation was over.

"I apologize, but I have to make a big deal out of this. Just between these four walls. Everywhere else, I will be as nonchalant as ever, I promise."

She paused, tapping her fingers on her legs.

"You know, I'm fairly certain that Alys trained with Duke Avery for a while in school. I believe she could make the introduction for you."

"Are you *trying* to kill me? Between the two of you, I will never live this down."

Vivienne leaned forward, grinning a lion's grin at me. I stared back at her and groaned.

"It's too late for regrets, my dear. You can't take it back now. Your father will be here with your sister in two weeks. In the meantime, I'm going to give you a refresher on how to be a proper lady."

"I already regret asking."

CORMAC

Finn was being a busybody, as usual. Whenever we had a large or difficult order come in, I tended to work overtime to make sure that everything got done as it needed to be. He had long since decided that it was his job to take care of me, and I hadn't stopped him. I knew that he worried about me, especially as we got further into the testing process for the swatches I had made. It was frustrating me to no end, and my language had gotten so bad that Poppy had banned me from their shop.

Their neighbors were much more genteel than mine had ever

pretended to be. Poppy hadn't disappeared, though. That was when they had taken to bringing some of their own work to the forge in the evenings, keeping up the quiet companionship while we worked.

Since we both had a tendency to get sucked into our work, Finn had decided that it was his responsibility to keep the both of us fed.

He had dragged us both out of the shop every night for the last week with increasingly silly excuses, ranging from needing help carrying something to thinking he'd seen a cat and wanted to catch it to wanting company to go see a show that just so happened to be at a restaurant Poppy had mentioned wanting to go to.

He was a good kid, but he wasn't as subtle as he thought he was. Poppy and I played along. While it wasn't technically Finn's job to make sure that we both ate regularly, I had to admit that it did tend to make his job easier in the long run.

A well-fed blacksmith was a happy blacksmith. A happy blacksmith was an easier master to work for, and tended to pay for his apprentice's meals.

Tonight was no different. I could see Finn trying to figure out an excuse to get us out of the shop.

"Where do you intend to drag us tonight, boy?" I growled good-naturedly, making Finn jump. "I'm fairly certain we've been to every ale house and bakery that's open late into the evening in the city in the last week. Or did you think you were being subtle?"

From where they sat behind me, Poppy leaned out and winked.

"I quite liked the bakery we went to a few days ago. Their game pie was delightful, and so artfully decorated! And their house ale wasn't bad, either. "

I rubbed a hand down my cheeks, stroking my full beard in thought.

"Is that the one that's a few streets over from the noble's

homes?" I wasn't as familiar with the city as Poppy was. They nodded.

"Let's go there for dinner," Poppy decided. "Come along, Finn. We'll feed you for your trouble."

"Let me grab my purse," I muttered.

"Come along, my fair fellows. Let's go find something to eat, shall we? And Cormac, leave the grousing to the hunters. We'll all work better on a full stomach." Poppy flounced out to the front room and waited while I ran back to my apartments to change my shirt and grab my money.

POPPY

After we'd been back from dinner for over an hour, metal clattered to the floor, followed swiftly by the sound of Cormac letting loose a string of curses that would have curled my mother's toes if she'd been there to hear it.

I raised my eyebrows at the man who was now hopping around on one foot.

"Is that language truly necessary? You're in polite company, remember?"

He scowled at me unrepentantly.

"As if your language would be any better if you dropped a slew of chainmail on those dainty feet of yours! D'you expect me to curtsy and thank it for falling on my toes?"

I simply waited, my mouth in a firm line that was not quite a smile or a frown. After a few heartbeats, he quit scowling and gingerly allowed his left foot to touch the ground again.

"Sorry."

"It's all right, dear. I know you're a bear when you're in pain.

But really, I wish you'd refrain from using such language where Finn and Isabel can hear you. I don't want them picking it up."

He stared at me for a moment, then his jaw went slack with astonishment.

"Finn and Isabel? They're both nearly full grown. And I'm sure this isn't the worst language they've ever heard."

I opened my mouth to reply but he waved a hand at me preemptively.

"*But* I'll keep my cursing to myself as much as possible. Sorry for offending, Poppy."

"That's all I ask. Now, would you like help with that chainmail or is it going to live on the floor now?"

He snorted.

"Oh, aye. I've decided to carpet the place in chainmail. That way, if anyone breaks in barefoot, they'll have a surprise coming to them."

I grinned at him. I loved it when he got sarcastic. It always led to him being his most ridiculous.

"Well, that sounds quite revolutionary. I'll be sure to tell the corner crier that you're entering a new business—arrow-proof floors! And in the meantime, I'll help you clean this up."

I rose, shaking the wrinkles out of my skirts, and walked across the smithy to him. Hiking them up so they wouldn't get dirty, I crouched against the packed dirt floor and lifted the edge of the garment he had been working on. It was heavier than I'd expected it to be.

I rose, pulling it with me and looking closely at the pattern that he had been working with the thin metal links. As the lamp light played off of their hammered surfaces, I realized that the pattern was not that different from the one I had been working on for a knitted lacework shawl for another client.

"Have you ever noticed the similarities between the pattern of your chainmail and a basic knit stitch?"

Cormac didn't answer me for a moment, taking the metal from my hands and laying it gently onto his work bench next to the wrenches he had been using before.

Beside him sat a wicker basket full of other, torso-sized swatches for Finn to test in the morning. Each one was a different weight so we could see exactly what size wire we needed to get the protection Ser Genevieve needed.

"No, but now that you mention it, the creation process isn't that different. Just replace the wrenches with knitting needles and it's about the same. I wonder if you even could knit with a thick wire like this..."

I was intrigued by the idea and kept thinking while he picked his tools up and went back to work.

"It's a bit less pliable than yarn would be, but I'm sure that it's possible. You could make some beautiful lacework jewelry like that, if you got really good at it."

He whirled around, his wrenches still in his hands, looking for all the world like a man who'd seen the Goddess. I hadn't even made it back to my chair and my own project yet.

"Poppy, you're a genius!"

"Yes, I am... but what have I done to deserve your praise this time?"

"I could knit these links to each other and make something that's lighter and more flexible without being horrifically heavy."

Oh. *Oh.*

"That might just work," I mused. "The wire would have to be pretty thick in order to hold up the chainmail and be as protective as it needs to be for Genevieve's purposes... but I think it's doable!"

He dropped his wrenches on the wood and crossed the room in two strides, his arms and his lips spread wide, making me feel welcomed. I could feel my mouth smile in reaction and my traitorous cheeks turn pink. I only hoped he couldn't see it in the ill light.

He grabbed me up and pulled me close to his chest, careful to avoid crushing me.

"I'm so glad I know you, Poppy. You are an absolute delight."

Now I was even more grateful he couldn't see my face. I could feel the heat reaching the tips of my ears.

When he let me go, I cleared my throat.

"You are a flatterer, my good sir."

He slapped a hand to his chest dramatically.

"I am no such thing! You wound me! When have I ever been accused of such a crime?"

"Well, right now, for one. I'm sure you've been accused of being a massive flirt before, you old coot."

A booming laugh burst out of his chest, one that I couldn't help but join him in. My soprano giggle intertwined with his baritone guffaw making music of our combined delight.

"I may have been called a massive flirt, but that's definitely the first time I've been called an old coot. Why can't you just take a compliment?"

He walked back to his work, still laughing. I made my way back to the chair I'd been working from.

"I can take a compliment!" I retorted.

"Just not from me, eh? I can stop if it makes you uncomfortable."

Even from across the room, I could see that he was chewing on the inside of his lip. I knew he would lay off the flirtatious banter if I told him to. But I wasn't sure that I wanted him to stop.

"No, it's all right, Cor," I told him, flashing him a small but sincere smile. "Thank you for the compliment."

"Thank you for being you, Poppy. I'm glad you're in my life. "

The sincerity and affection he felt for me was clear in his voice. It washed over me and I felt the same feelings for him rush through me.

We had been friends for a long time. Lately, though, it seemed as if he wanted something slightly different than my friendship. And I enjoyed the changes to our banter. It was a little more flirtatious and I got to see all the parts of Cormac that I didn't usually. But I didn't know if I was ready to potentially change the path our relationship would take for the rest of our lives.

If we tried out a romantic relationship and it didn't work, I was worried about how we would go back to the closeness we'd shared since he moved to the capital.

At the same time, I wondered what it would be like to be held romantically again, and by someone I cared for so deeply already.

Looking at his large gentle hands and his sweet smile under a rough but tamed black beard, I couldn't help but imagine what it would be like to have sex with the much larger man.

Biting my lip, I turned back to my work. Those were things I needed to save thinking about for later.

3

CORMAC

I had spent the last two weeks adjusting to knitting with heavy wire. It had been frustrating at first because of the strength needed to twist the metal into the shape that I needed, and then because of the sheer amount of wire that I had wound up needing. Finn had gone all over the city buying up the right gauge of wire, and we still hadn't had enough to finish the swatch to test to see if this would even work.

I never thought I'd be grateful to my granddam for teaching me to knit when I was a boy, but here I sat in Poppy's well-lit shop. My wrists were killing me from the strain of the repetitive motion, and Finn had made more wire than I'd ever tasked him with in the four years he'd been my apprentice.

But finally, we were almost finished with what would be the torso section of Ser Genevieve's gown. If this didn't work, we were back to the beginning and I might wind up having to tell the knight that we couldn't make this work. But if it did... we might be on to something great.

I finished the end of a row and counted. We had enough to be usable for a test.

"Finn, my boy! I am ready for you!"

The boy, nearly a full grown man by now, jerked awake from the lounge chair where he had been dozing.

"Huh? Wha-?" he blinked rapidly. I could almost see the cogs in his brain starting to turn as he actually woke up. Poppy laughed and the ringing sound was like music to my ears. Finn's ears turned pink from what I could only guess was embarrassment.

"Time to wake up. It's your turn to test this out."

Poppy set down their work and together we waited. Finn started the now familiar routine of setting up for a test. He rolled his shoulders in an attempt to loosen them from the day's work and his uncomfortable sleep position. It was a very different workout swinging a sword at chain mail instead of his usual hammering at the forge.

Finn was nearly old enough to enroll in the army if he'd wanted to, but I suspected that if there was a war both of our skills as blacksmiths would be more useful than anything we could provide as soldiers. I knew he had been enjoying playing with the swords, axes and crossbows as part of our testing method.

Today we were using a longsword, because Poppy's shop didn't have enough room to do a full swing of an axe without breaking anything, or the right range for a crossbow.

Finn pulled it from the sheath he had laid on the floor next to him. I nodded approvingly as he oiled the length of the blade from tip to hilt and then wiped it clean again.

He placed the blade on the table we'd made our staging area and adjusted the leather mannequin so that it was centered in the room. I draped the chain mail cloth around its neck and torso and nodded at him before getting out of the way.

Rolling his shoulders one more time for good measure, Finn picked up the sword and settled into a battle stance. He spread his feet to balance himself on the packed dirt floor, and turned himself slightly sideways. He looked carefully at the mannequin, as if he were aiming for the places that an enemy would most likely strike in a real battle.

Please let this work. Please let this work, I thought.

"Would you like to try, sir?" Finn asked hesitantly, sword in hand.

I shook my head and smiled.

"I'll let you put those young arms to use."

Finn grinned and focused on the mannequin.

Five well-placed blows later, he stepped back and wiped a bead of sweat from his forehead with the back of his gloves. Grabbing a lantern from the wall behind him, he looked carefully at the chain mail. I stepped up behind him, another lantern in my hand so we could see every facet of the swatch of knitted chainmail.

We stood in silence, looking hard at the fabric. Several rings glinted where the sword had struck them, but none of the rings had detached. None of them were even terribly damaged.

"Well, did it work?" Poppy asked from their chair.

"We just might have done it," I whispered, awestruck. Raising my voice, I called to Poppy. "Come and take a look for yourself!"

They walked briskly into the room a moment later, and both Finn and I stepped out of the way for them to take a long hard look.

They gestured with two fingers at Finn, and he stared at them blankly for a moment before handing over his lantern. Stripping the glove off of their right hand, they ran their pinky finger and the side of their hand down the cloth a few times.

They turned slowly, an expression of abject delight on their face.

"Cormac, Finn, you did it! This is more or less undamaged! We can make this gown!"

They grabbed me around the waist and squeezed as tight as they could. I let my hands rest on their shoulders and they began to laugh.

"We really did it," I said wonderingly. Proud tears had begun to well in my eyes, and I wasn't the least bit ashamed. "Well, ain't that a thing."

I gestured for Finn to come closer, and he did, setting his lantern on the table next to the sword. I wrapped him in my arms right next to Poppy, happy to have them both as part of my team.

"Ain't that a thing," I whispered.

<hr>

GENEVIEVE

"You want me to do what now?"

Alys looked so much like our mother in that moment. Her blonde eyebrows arched into her artificially bright orange hairline incredulously and her Cupid's bow lips were spread into a smirk that would have been appropriate for a mustache-twirling villain at the theater. I hated that smirk.

"Oh, come on, Alys, it's just an introduction! That wouldn't be so bad, right?"

Alys laughed.

"You need *me* to do something for *you*? I don't think this has ever happened before, sister dear."

I grimaced. She was right. It was rare for me to ask either of my siblings for help.

"Yeah, it's been that kind of a season. Just tell me, can you help me or not? Mama thought you might be able to, but if it's an imposition..."

"What, you'll just die lonely? Is Duke Avery the only man in the world for you?"

She faked a swoon mockingly.

"Oh my goddess, Alys, don't be ridiculous!" I snapped, pinching the bridge of my nose between my thumb and forefinger in annoyance. "This is why I don't ask you for things. You make a big production out of everything."

"You're the one asking me to introduce you to the Duke, like you aren't in the same position I am at court, if not a better one," Alys shot back. "Seriously, this is the first crush you've ever mentioned to me, and it's on the King's scandalous son."

"Look, you know Duke Avery. You went to school with him. You're going to the same ball I am, and several others besides. Is it too much to ask for you to talk to your old friend and say, 'Hey, you should meet my sister'?"

I could hear my voice rising an octave with each sentence I spoke and I hated it, but there was nothing I could do about it.

"And what if he says no? What if he's not into women or not into anyone at all? What will you do then?"

"I'll survive," I nearly screeched. Taking a deep breath to calm myself, I continued. "I don't need a man to be happy in my life, and if he's not interested, then he's not interested. That'll be that and I'll move on."

I flopped onto the bench in the hallway with a huff. There would be no convincing her.

"If you don't want to do it, that's fine. Just tell me and we'll be done with it. I'm done arguing with you about this."

Alys was silent for several heartbeats before gathering her skirts around herself and sitting gracefully next to me.

"That was pretty bratty of me, wasn't it?"

I only snorted, shifting away slightly. My sister sighed, and I felt the air move as she ran her fingers through her fiery hair.

"I got caught up in the moment a little bit."

"No kidding. We're both adults now. I thought we were done acting like little kids, Alys. There's no reason for it."

The younger woman squirmed in her seat before she spoke again.

"You're right. I'm sorry. I'll talk to Avery for you. I was always going to."

"Then why... You know what, never mind. Thank you, Alys. Let me know when and where I need to be to meet him. I'm going to go practice with the guards."

I rose from the bench, walking into my open bedroom without another word. Closing the door behind me, I pressed my forehead against it for good measure.

My face was hot against the cool wood of the door, and I could feel the texture of the grain in every wrinkle in my forehead. I took deep breaths that were supposed to be calming. I wasn't sure if it was working or not, but I felt like I could breathe easier after a few of them.

I could never figure out why every request I made of my sister turned into an argument. As far as I could remember, it had always been like this. I almost wished I'd asked Mama to make the request for me, but at least it was over for now.

Pulling myself away from the door, I began unfastening the side clasp of the simple dress I wore. I intended to go practice with the guards Papa had brought with them. It would help to beat out the worries that were floating around my consciousness. Until my new gown was finished, practice required trousers.

AVERY

My mother and I had been to three balls already this week, and it was only Thursday. I had yet to see any of my former classmates or fellow scholars at these balls, and I was starting to get cranky about the inordinate amounts of time that I was wasting.

It had turned out to be convenient for Bayard and Ines to have two people who could attend balls with similar social standing to their own as stand-ins for them. My mother had been happy to accept their well-planned pleading requests, but I had no choice but to stand in for my father, who had declared that he had had enough balls for three lifetimes during his reign.

So there I stood, back to the wall and desperately wishing that I had thought to bring a book with me, when a familiar voice called out from the throng of silk-clad nobles.

"Why, Duke Avery of Wolvington! I should have known to check the corners when I couldn't find you."

A fiery-haired woman dressed in green and black silk stepped forward from the crowd. A lazy smile spread across her painted lips and I couldn't help but grin back.

"Alys of Teagan. It has been far too long."

I meant it. She presented her hand to me politely and I clasped it warmly, pulling her into an impromptu hug that she returned with a ringing laugh.

"It's good to see you again," she told me, sincerity clear in her voice. "I wasn't sure when I'd actually get to see you this season, but if King Bayard can't seem to get time away from his dealings with the Fraisians, at least we get to see more of you."

"I don't see how I'm much of an asset at a party like this, but it's good to see you, too. I was just lamenting my lack of a novel to dive into."

She smirked at me.

"How about we go grab a drink instead? I've got something I want to talk to you about."

"Is that so? Ladies first, then!" I laughed.

She led the way through the astonishing number of well-dressed dancing nobles, straight for the bar. I was surprised to see my mother standing there, happily chatting with Duchess Vivienne of Teagan. That was unusual. My mother was usually surrounded by groups of noblewomen looking to curry favor with her as the wife of the King Father.

Duchess Vivienne didn't need any help that Father would be able to do anything for. She had enough clout on her own. So why were she and my mother talking like old friends?

Alys cleared her throat and both women turned to her.

"Alys, my dear girl! You found him!" Mother cried.

I narrowed my eyes. Something odd was going on here. I bowed.

"Hello again, Mother. Your Grace, it is a pleasure to see you again."

Duchess Vivienne dipped a light curtsy. My mother just smiled at me.

"The same to you, dear boy! I've just been discussing your marriage prospects with your dear mother."

"Is that so?"

"Yes. I understand that you are interested in a potential arranged marriage? I had a candidate in mind if that is the case."

Raising an eyebrow, I turned to Alys in surprise.

"If you were looking to get married, you could have just asked me yourself. I wouldn't have said yes, but..."

"Ew!" she cried, swatting me playfully. "Don't be gross, you're my teacher. We're not here to talk about me."

I scratched at my cheek and frowned in confusion. If they weren't here to talk about Alys, then why were she and the Duchess involved? Alys rolled her eyes at me.

"My older sister, Genevieve, has expressed an interest. You've met a few times."

I vaguely remembered her as a tall and muscular woman with tanned skin and brown hair that she kept braided. We had talked a few times over the course of Alys's time studying with me and I had enjoyed each conversation, but I hadn't given her much thought since Alys had graduated from the Academy in the fall.

"It would be an acceptable political match," Mother said. "The Duchess said that your terms would not be a problem in their house."

"I would not be opposed to such a match," I offered tentatively. "I would like to spend some time with her, though. I don't want to marry someone who I can't talk to."

Vivienne chuckled and exchanged a knowing look with Mother.

"I see why you've been having trouble finding him a wife," she joked. "Lucky for him, Genevieve is just as difficult. I think we can make that happen."

Mother's eyes gleamed as she nodded to me. Maybe the social season would be more exciting than I had anticipated.

4

———

GENEVIEVE

I rubbed my thumb and forefinger over my eyebrows, trying not to scream. We had been at this all morning. My mother seemed to be intent on me learning everything that I had failed to learn in my etiquette classes in one day. I desperately wanted someone to come in and interrupt, but I knew no one would. Mama had made sure to tell the servants not to interrupt us unless it was urgent, and Papa had taken Peter to go see a new artist in town.

"Oh, for the Goddess's sake, Gen, you know how to walk properly," my mother wailed, slumping back in the overstuffed chair she favored. "You walk like a Knight, which is fine, but it is not sexually appealing in the least. Most of the art of seduction is in your body language and you are giving me *nothing* to work with."

Honestly, I wanted to learn it, too. It had all seemed so silly in class, and it definitely still was, but it was a weapon that I didn't have in my arsenal. Not to mention, I knew I needed all the help I could get. The knighthood process might have been opened to all genders more than a century ago, but it was still very traditionally masculine when it came to etiquette.

That was why Mama had enrolled me in etiquette classes designed for noblewomen. Except none of it had stuck. There had been enough overlap that I had gotten away with a lot over the years, but flirting was not covered in either of those classes.

Alys burst into the room carrying a massive pile of fluffy material.

"Mama, I've got just the thing. No one can resist being sexy in this!"

She lifted her arms and revealed that the mass of light pink fabric in her hands was, in fact, a very puffy skirt. I backed away, hands up in front of me.

"Oh no. No way am I wearing that."

Alys shook the fabric at me and I shuddered.

"It would just be for practice," she laughed. "You wouldn't have to wear it out in public."

"There's just so much of it," I whispered in horror. "I don't even know how you would walk in that."

Alys laughed a little.

"I will have you know that this is one of the latest fashions from Fraisia," she told me in her loftiest voice. "It will even make you look like you have hips!"

"My hips work perfectly well, thank you very much," I retorted, making my point clear by placing my fists on them.

"Yes, and they blend in with your extremely muscled torso," she explained patiently. "This will give you a more feminine shape to work with. It has built in shapers that will move with you while expanding your silhouette."

As she explained the garment's unique details to me, I saw what she was talking about.

"You know, this might actually work," Mama said brightly. Alys beamed over her shoulder at her and then turned her gleaming eyes on me. I threw my hands up in the air. I knew when I had been defeated.

"Fine. I'll change into that skirt. Give me five minutes," I grumbled.

Alys squealed and tossed it to me. I hid my smile behind the skirt's many layers. I dug through them, trying to find the waistband and how it fastened. It looked as complicated as any corset I'd ever seen.

"Can you help me with it? I'm not entirely sure how to actually get into this," I admitted.

"I'm right behind you. I knew it was a two person job."

Of course she had. Together, we bustled into the sitting room and closed the door behind us. We fell into a familiar rhythm. Alys and I had spent a lot of time helping each other in and out of various costumes and outfits when we were younger, but I couldn't remember the last time we'd asked each other for help.

"All right, let's get you out of this gown, then. You'll be fine in your shift with this, if you're comfortable with that?"

"As long as you don't have any other surprises in store for me this afternoon, that's fine. Now help me move this table out of the way."

Together, we shoved the coffee table out of the way enough for me to stand in the middle of the room.

"Nope, this is it. And I swore I'd only use it if you needed it."

"Oh, so you had this planned?"

I'd have been upset if I hadn't suspected it. She laughed and began unlacing the stays at the back of my form-fitting plaid gown.

"Sort of? I'd gotten this for you anyway and it sounded like you could use a rescuer."

I grimaced. She wasn't wrong. Mama and I had been on the verge of actually fighting for the first time in years after several hours of struggling.

"Thanks for that. I'm not doing as well at this as I'd like. But, really, is the way you *walk* that important?" I huffed. Alys laughed lightly at me as she set up the skirt for me to be able to step into. She held the flexible leather inserts apart so I wouldn't scrape my legs while I covered myself.

"It's like learning a new style of fighting. You have to get the basics down before you can do anything else. Walking is one of the basics. You'll get there. It took me weeks to have Mama approve my posture and walking style."

"Yeah, when you were *seven*. I'm a grown woman. I should be able to figure this out."

I knew she was rolling her eyes behind me.

"Yes, well, we all come to these things at different times. You're learning something new. Quit beating yourself up. And suck in your stomach just a little. This needs to be tight."

I did as I was told, closing my eyes and holding my breath while she laced the skirt around me. It was comfortable, even with the leather shaping inserts. When Alys told me to let out my breath, I looked down at myself and my next breath was nearly a gasp. The layers of silk and cotton draped beautifully over the inserts and my thighs. It gave me just the hint of the curves that were so prominent on my mother and siblings. It left me feeling breathless in a way that had nothing to do with the stays.

I twirled the skirt, letting it flare out around me and giggling. I caught sight of Alys grinning shyly, twisting her body back and forth as she looked me up and down. Without thinking, I grabbed her up in my arms and squeezed her. She held herself very still for a moment before softening and wrapping her arms around me. Her cheek pressed to mine and I felt her smile.

"Thank you, Alys. This means a lot."

"I'm glad you like it, Genevieve. Now, let's get back out there and help you learn how to flirt."

We released each other and smiled widely. A sense of calm washed over me that had been missing all day. I could do this.

CORMAC

The back room of Poppy's shop flooded with light when the door creaked open, only to be filled with a dark shadow. We both turned to see Finn lumber into the room we'd been holed up in for what felt like an eternity trying to put the finishing touches onto the gown for Ser Genevieve. Even with help from our apprentices, we'd spent the last two weeks crafting enough chainmail and knitting it into the right shapes to make the dress as protective as it needed to be.

Finn struggled to carry a leather satchel as he walked across the too-bright room, even for the strong apprentice.

"Ser Genevieve's men delivered her ornamental pauldrons, sir. And lord, they're heavy!"

I cursed, shoving a pile of finished chainmail pieces to the side of the table so that he could set the satchel down. He lowered it carefully, then rolled his shoulders to relax the muscles.

Resting his hands on the satchel once he had stretched, he looked to me for permission to open it.

At my nod, he lifted the top layer of the dark leather by its fraying seams. I slid the simple wooden box from the interior, emptying the bag. Finn pulled the leather away and placed it on the floor next to the table, leaving me to look over the pauldrons inside it. Poppy slid into the space he'd left behind, inspecting the stitchwork on the limp bag with a hawkish glare.

"She needs a better leatherworker," they sighed. "This is shoddy work."

"I'm sure this is just one of their delivery bags, Poppy," Finn laughed. "Look at how weathered it is. It looks like it's almost as old as I am."

"Its stitches should still hold together better than that, no matter the age," they sniffed, planting their hands on their wide hips. "You ought to know that, boy. What would have happened if any two of these fraying stitches had fallen apart? Those pretty pauldrons would have been on the ground for anyone to grab up."

I rolled my eyes, knowing this was just the beginning of another one of their bickering matches. They had become more common between all three of us as our nerves got frayed.

"What are the chances of the right two stitches coming apart right when it needed to be in use?"

"With shoddy stitchwork like this? Significantly higher than you would expect. Are you gonna keep telling me how stitches work, youngling? I will win every time."

I turned to them just in time to see Poppy raise their thick eyebrows combatively and to hear Finn laugh in response.

"You're right, of course. You would know better."

"Yeah, Poppy keeps us all in stitches," I joined in with a wink. "Now come here, boy. I want to show you these pieces of art."

Finn's eyes lit up when he saw the pauldrons I had laid out on the table. Poppy was no more than two steps behind him, and they let out a low whistle.

The largest base of each pauldron was perfectly polished steel, with a chevron of carved brass overlay. The oak leaves that were central to the Teagan crest were carved lovingly into the brass. I turned them so that Finn could see the interior leather that would press against Ser Genevieve's shoulder, running a finger along the nearly nonexistent seam.

"It's beautiful," he sighed.

"That, my boy, is what skill looks like. Even I can't work this finely, and I've been at this a long, long time."

"And, they'll be the perfect addition to this gown!"

Poppy clapped their hands and looked over to the mannequin they'd been using to put the dress together piece by piece. They motioned to me to bring them over. Cradling one pauldron in my large, callused hands, I walked carefully across the room to the mannequin that held the mostly completed gown. Poppy fluttered around me, guiding my hands so I could place the pauldrons on its metal shoulders properly.

Finn gasped at the effect that the addition made and I could see why. Even without the second one attached, it pulled the entire gown together. This went from being a chainmail and silk gown to a gown fit for a lady knight, from the bronze chainmail links in the bodice that matched the oak leaf pattern on the pauldron to the bright steel that was hidden in the deep blue skirt.

I was blown away by the way the dress looked. I could only imagine what it would look like on Ser Genevieve's sturdy frame. I had never given much thought to how women looked in ball gowns, but I knew it would be stunning. I almost couldn't believe I'd had a hand in creating it.

"Well, let's get back to work! We've got a gown to finish!" Poppy declared, breaking the hush that had fallen over the room.

Finn and I grinned and went back to work. It was time to gather all of the chainmail pieces and do a final quality check before they were attached to the gown.

AVERY

The entire family was gathered around the private dining table in the royal quarters.

I sliced into my meat, minding my own business and hoping that I wouldn't be drawn into the debate of how to solve the trade problems we were having with Fraisia. My niblings, Julian and Cecilia, sat on either side of me doing the same. It was bad enough that we all had to deal with these discussions during the day, but it didn't have to be our dinner conversation as well. My opinion was not one that my brother and father agreed with.

A chill ran up my spine as I felt someone's eyes on me. Looking around the table, I caught my cousin Cedric's eagle eyes focused on me.

"I hear you've been having some trouble with wolves out in Wolvington. Seems appropriate for the name."

I snorted. He was right, even if he did look and sound like a villain from a novel, waving his fork around like an extension of his body.

"I've asked my soldiers to shoot any wolves they see on sight, since they really shouldn't be seeing them. Hopefully that will help fix the problems we've been having."

"Any idea why they've been attacking? It's been a relatively mild winter and your forests are flush with game and goats. I can't imagine they're hungry."

"Honestly, I have no idea, but it's driving my seneschal mad. Were lucky they haven't gone into any of the villages, honestly."

"Do you need help dealing with them? I'd be happy to send a few knights your way."

Shrugging, I put another bite of food into my mouth, using the time that I was chewing to corral my thoughts.

"I think that my soldiers can handle it for now. We've only had a few attacks and they haven't been particularly severe. But I'll keep that in mind if we find ourselves overwhelmed."

"You do that. There's no sense in letting your people get injured when I have a gaggle of bored knights bouncing around balls and things. Speaking of, I hear you have a date planned."

At that, everyone at the table's eyes fixed on me. Suppressing a groan, I had to nod. This was happening, whether I liked it or not.

"With one of your knights, actually. I don't know how it's going to go yet, so don't get your hopes up." That was directed at the entire table, and seemed to be a cue for my mother to open her mouth. As usual, she took over the conversation, gesturing with a delicate hand.

"Tell me, how well do you know this Ser Genevieve of Teagan? She has a good reputation around town."

I wanted a hole to open up precisely underneath my feet and somehow suck me into it without harming anyone else. Was it realistic? No. But if it would get me out of this discussion, it might be worth whatever havoc it would wreak on life at the palace. I didn't even care where I'd wind up, really. Anywhere would be better than here right at this moment.

* * *

CORMAC

I had a problem. I had run out of things that I could work on away from the forge. Everything else required high heat, or too many tools to make it feasible to bring with me to Poppy's workshop. But the gown Poppy was working on was now too bulky and unfinished to be dragging back and forth down the avenue between our shops. I had to find a reason for Poppy and I to keep spending time together. I had been racking my brain for ways to do that all evening but everything I came up with just sounded contrived and ridiculous.

"What would you say if I asked you out to dinner?" I blurted unthinkingly. It took a Herculean effort to keep me from clapping my hands over my mouth as they stared at me.

Instead, I cleared my throat and then continued. "A romantic dinner. Just us two."

I just looked at them, waiting for them to respond. They sunk into the chair that they had been working from before replying.

"I think that that would be... kind of nice? Can we be lovers and friends? I don't want anything that happens in the bedroom, or not, to affect this."

They waved a hand between the two of us, and I caught it, rubbing a calloused thumb gently over the tips of their work worn fingers.

"I'm not looking for anything more than you're willing to offer. If you're not ready for a more romantic relationship, or decide that you don't want a romantic relationship, I will not be hurt or upset. I just want you to know that."

The smile spread across the rest of their golden brown face, and they stood to walk back over to where I sat.

I smiled, noticing that we were almost the same height - when I was sitting down. I wasn't used to being face-to-face with Poppy, instead of looking down at the top of their head all the time. Their brown eyes glittered with an emotion I could not quite identify.

"Do you think that is what you want?" I asked, as gently as I could. "Want to give romance a try with me in addition to our friendship?"

They stood there, looking at me for what felt like hours but was certainly only a few of my racing heartbeats. They bit their lips and leaned forward, resting their hands on the arms of my chair.

"Why don't you lean forward and kiss me and find out?"

Instead, I stood quickly, sweeping them up in my arms so we were the same height. Their legs dangled around my knees, and they giggled.

"Cormac! That was unexpected!"

I looked at them seriously. Their giggles subsided and they bit their lightly painted lip as they looked at my mouth, then back up at my eyes.

"May I kiss you, Poppy?"

"You may."

And so I did.

5

I stood half-dressed before the looking glass in my bedroom. My crisp teal shirt was half buttoned over the whalebone undershirt that helped to shape my upper body. One of the servants have helped me get into it earlier in the morning, and I had tucked the tails into my unbuckled dark trousers. Something about my appearance was off today but I couldn't quite put my finger on it and it was frustrating.

One of the problems with changing my body's appearance little by little was that my physicians and I had to go incredibly slowly with each spell, making changes over years. Making changes too quickly only led to migraines and spells going awry in ways that were time consuming and painful to fix. But something was *off* in one of the spells and I wasn't sure what it was. A wrinkle that felt as deep as a canyon spread across my forehead as I mentally cataloged each of the different spells wrapped around my body, from the one that slowly widened my jawbone to be more striking to the major internal spell that adjusted my hormones. As far as I could tell, everything was in working order. I loved the way each of them glittered in their own way. It was beautiful.

The clock in the nearby tower tolled two hours past noon and I cursed. I was going to be more than fashionably late if I didn't leave immediately. I was going to have to deal with whatever was bothering me throughout the meal. Buttoning the teal shirt, I added a silver necklace that trailed down my chest. It brightened my brown skin and made me feel a little bit better about this lunch. I buckled my trousers and slid my stockinged feet into the black shoes that closed with a delicate silver clasp that matched the necklace.

Once I was fully put together, I took one last look in the mirror. Maybe whatever was bothering me was just something with the lighting in the room Bayard had assigned me.

It could have also had something to do with the butterflies I had in my stomach. I was always anxious about new people, and most of what I knew about Genevieve was from our few short meetings and the stories I'd heard over the years as Alys's mentor. I couldn't help but wonder how the real woman would stack up to the one that my student had told me about.

Would I actually feel a spark? Did it matter if I did? Arranged marriages like the one our families had discussed at the ball two weeks prior didn't require it, but they did require respect for one another. But I wanted more than that. I wanted a partner who would be my equal and who I could genuinely enjoy relaxing around. Maybe a spark was too much to ask for, but I wanted it anyway. And now it was time to go see if it was possible.

I grabbed a cloak to ward off the chill of the spring air and swept out of the room.

GENEVIEVE

Avery was late and I was fairly certain I was going to lose my mind. What if he wasn't coming? I couldn't stop my knee from bouncing till it almost hit the table. Alys pressed her palm to my knee and I could feel the heat of it through my mulberry silk gown. Unable to bounce with her hands there, I traced my fingers over the wood grain of the table in an attempt to use my nervous energy.

"It's going to be fine, Gen," Alys snapped. "Quit bouncing like a rabbit."

She had set us up for a late lunch at a restaurant that we had both come to think of as a favorite in the last few years. While the Royal Academy where Alys had trained until recently was not in Caerleon proper, it was close enough that she had spent nearly every break and weekend in the city flirting with anyone she found interesting.

I may have been the one wearing armor on a regular basis, but Alys had always been braver when it came to social events and strangers - something I'd always envied her for. I wished that I wasn't so anxious, but Avery was nearly half an hour late. I couldn't stand for people to be late for exactly this reason, even if he was royalty.

Right when I opened my mouth to say so, I caught a flash of teal out of the corner of my eye. Alys's fingers dug into my leg, and I knew that he was here.

"That's his favorite shirt," she whispered, raising her thin eyebrows at me. "He must be aiming to impress someone today."

Duke Avery of Wolvington wove through the collection of tables and chairs gracefully. When he had a clear path to the corner table we'd been placed at, Alys and I stood. She was rock solid, but I felt like my knees were made of jelly, from nerves and from the heat I felt in the pit of my stomach. The man was *handsome.*

Get it together, Genevieve, I told myself. *It's just a man, even if he is the most handsome man you've ever seen. There is no need for you to fall apart.*

I felt a hand intertwined with mine and looked over at my sister. She had a kind smile on her face, as if she could tell what I was thinking. It was nice to see that smile directed at me for once, but it was still strange.

Duke Avery was dressed beautifully and I couldn't help but stare as he walked towards us. The teal that I had seen was his shirt, decorated with a large but delicate silver necklace that accented the timepiece he wore on his wrist.

He caught my gaze and winked. Heat rushed to my cheeks so quickly that I had to resist the urge to press my hands to them to check if they were on fire. My gaze dropped to the floor and I took several deep breaths.

I can only hope that I was making as good an impression on him as he was on me. I knew that I looked good, even if I could hardly stand on my own from swooning.

You have faced down trolls and fae with nary a quaver, I reminded myself. This *is what gets your knees quaking? Don't be ridiculous. You can handle this.*

By the time he made it to the table, I was able to stand on my own without holding onto the table. Given the state I had been in since he arrived, that was something to be proud of.

"Alys, it's wonderful to see you again! I was so happy to hear from you!" His voice was light and sincere, with a light burr that made me suddenly homesick. "And you must be Genevieve. It's a pleasure to actually meet you."

Surreptitiously wiping my palms on the insides of my pockets, I shook his hand. His grip was firm, but not crushing, and his hands were softer than I expected. Then again, I wasn't used to shaking hands with men who didn't spend their entire lives building up muscles and calluses with weapons practice. My gaze traveled from his hands up his flat chest to his slightly stubbly chin, catching at the sight of his plumped lips spread in a wide smile. The grin showed a thin gap between his front teeth, and I realized belatedly that I needed to say something.

"The pleasure is all mine, Duke Avery."

He raised an eyebrow at me.

"Oh please, just call me Avery. There's no need to be formal. We're all equals here, are we not?"

"Absolutely, of course." I blushed again and nodded.

"Now that you two have met, shall we eat?" Alys interrupted. "I've been looking forward to this meal all week."

"Yes, yes. I'd like to use the restroom first. If the waiter comes while I'm not at the table, ask for a lemonade for me, would you, Alys?

"Sure thing!" She smiled at her old friend, who walked towards the back of the restaurant. As soon as he was out of sight, she whirled on me, her bewilderment plain on her face.

"Will you act like a human being? He's not that scary!"

"I'm terrible at this! I don't know why I thought this was a good idea. Maybe I should just go?"

Alys's eyebrows rose to her hairline.

"Are you kidding me? You'll do fine, if you can figure out how to make some small talk and get more comfortable around each other."

"What do you mean 'around each other?' He's not nervous at all! He was winking and joking with you."

"That's because he knows me. He doesn't know you at all, and you're not giving him anything to work with. He could tell that you were nervous which is why he went to the bathroom before the meal. That's him giving you space to breathe, you gooseberry."

I blinked a few times, thinking through what her sister had

said before speaking. She must have known his behavior patterns on dates better than I'd anticipated.

"Oh."

"'Oh' is right. We talked about this before we came, remember? He likes books and learning about things he doesn't know anything about. You like books, and you know a lot of random stuff. You can talk to him, Gen. It's not as hard as you're making it out to be in your head. Oh, here comes the waiter."

Alys went from lecturing me to chattering with the waiter about the special of the day - suckling pig with carrots, turnips and potatoes - and how his day was going so far. It was an impressively quick change of topic. She ordered a round of lemonades for the table. Once the waiter left to go find their drinks, I changed the topic again.

"Have you found your dress yet for the Prince's ball?"

Alys sighed, leaning back in her chair discontentedly.

"Not yet. Father's brought us to town so late that it's been difficult to find a tailor that's actually able to take on another dress."

"Would you like me to ask Poppy if they're able to take on another gown? Mine is set to be delivered tomorrow, and as far as I know, they don't have any other gowns to make for this year's ball."

Alys's entire face brightened.

"Oh, do you think they'd be able to make it happen? I have a couple of options from the tailors back home, but they're not nearly as skilled as the tailors here. Plus, their shop sounds wonderful to just be in. Could we go and visit them?"

"I'm pretty booked up this evening, but I think they're to deliver my surprise gown tomorrow afternoon. I can ask them then?"

She clapped her hands in delight at the suggestion.

"That would be wonderful, Gen! I wouldn't have thought to

ask them, what with your gown being such a project on its own. I don't want to overload them at the last minute."

I shrugged.

"It can't hurt to ask, at the very least. The worst they can do is say no, right?"

Alys nodded, and then nearly jumped out of her chair when a dark hand clapped her around the shoulder.

"Avery, you cad!" She cried. "It's not nice to scare people like that."

He laughed, a deep, booming laugh that brought light into his deep brown eyes and sent a jolt of desire to my nether regions.

"Sorry, Alys! I couldn't resist. It was such a good opportunity. Ah, and I believe those are our drinks!"

Indeed they were. The waitress set the drinks in front of each of us, to a grateful chorus. She left us to our menus.

"So, Avery," Genevieve started. He looked over his menu at me expectantly and I faltered for a moment.

Come on. You are a perfectly good conversationalist. Show it.

I started again, keeping my eyes on my menu.

"Alys tells me that you are an avid reader. What have you been reading recently?"

I peeked up at him. His brown eyes lit up and he leaned towards me to tell me about his latest book.

AVERY

By the end of the meal, the three of us were alternating between roaring with laughter at each other's jokes and falling into deep conversations about esoteric topics. I was honestly surprised by how much fun I was having. Genevieve was a delightful woman, full of stories of life at the palace and everywhere her squiredom to Ser Raoul had taken her.

"I hope you all enjoyed the meal," the waitress said cheerily. "We also have a delightful lemon meringue pie with our own shortbread crust and a raspberry flummery, if anyone is interested in a dessert this afternoon."

We all demurred, though both sounded delicious. I gave the waitress my full attention.

"I don't think I could eat another bite," I laughed, rubbing my stomach. "Thank you very much, darling. And I'll have the check for all three of us, if you please."

She curtsied, offering me the small slip of paper. Nodding at the price, I pulled my purse out and paid her with four large bronze coins.

"Keep the change."

She beamed back at me, curtsied and collected the rest of our dishes from the table. I felt something brush my foot under the table. I looked under it just in time to see Alys stomp hard on Genevieve's foot. I raised an eyebrow at the both of them.

"Is there a problem?"

"No, of course not!" Alys beamed. Genevieve just shook her head. "That meal was one of the best I've had since I've arrived. I don't think I've ever had suckling pig prepared quite that well."

I had to agree that the meal had been wonderful. Especially since I had had lovely company to accompany the delicious food.

"That pie was heavenly, wasn't it, Genevieve?"

We had both ordered the fisherman's pie. It had been delicious and filling, with three different kinds of fish, spring onions, mussels and scallops under a bed of mashed parsley and potatoes.

"I've lived in this city my whole life, and I've never had anything quite that good," she admitted, her cheeks pink.

"What, they don't feed you that well at the palace every day? I'll have to tell the King's cook that they need to raise the bar for you knights." I punctuated the joke with a wink. We both knew that the cooks at the palace wouldn't be changing their regular menu for the knights, even for a half-royal Duke.

Her mouth quirked up into a lopsided smile that made my heart stutter. I don't know how I had never noticed just how pretty Genevieve was before today. Scratch that. I did know. I had been so focused on what Alys needed and my studies that I had barely glanced her way. It was a shame, because now that I had her company, I didn't want the day to end. I racked my brain, trying to think of ways that I could spend more time with her without being overly aggressive about it. Then I realized, I had seen the perfect thing on the way over.

Focusing my attention on Genevieve's bright eyes, I grinned.

"I saw a new bookseller's cart in town. Would you ladies care to accompany me?"

Genevieve glanced sideways to her sister, who was already shaking her head tragically.

"Alas, I have a very important meeting to attend, but you two should go together! I'm sure Genevieve hasn't finished her shopping for my birthday, and there's bound to be something suitable at your bookseller's."

It was Alys's turn to wink at Genevieve. I leaned over and grabbed my own satchel, trying to hide the smile on my face, not wanting them to know I'd seen this show of sisterly affection.

"You two go and have fun. I'll take care of the business with the accountant. I haven't been scolded by Ianto for years! It will be fun."

I stood, and both Alys and Genevieve echoed the movement.

"My old friend, it will be disappointing to shop without you, but I hope you do have fun with the accountant. I'm not sure I've ever said those particular words in that order, but they're true nonetheless. My good ser, would you do me the honor of accompanying me on this trip?"

I offered Genevieve my arm, and she accepted it with a stately curtsy. A spark raced straight to my heart from the contact. Alys watched, pride clear in her eyes.

"I believe our carriage shall be here momentarily, Ser Genevieve. Shall we wait outside?"

She smiled up at me and it was like looking into the sun and I never wanted it to set.

"That would be lovely."

Alys waved at both of them as they walked away, arm in arm.

GENEVIEVE

The carriage ride to the bookseller's stall was short, but comfortable. People tended to get out of the way for carriages, especially those marked with the royal family's seal. It was also quiet, or as quiet as a horse-drawn carriage ride could be on a cobblestone road in the middle of the city. Avery and I were taking turns looking out the window of the carriage and glancing at each other when we thought the other person wasn't looking. I knew that my cheeks were pink, but I didn't care, because I could see similar spots of pink on his high cheekbones. Before it had fully stopped, he swung himself out and onto the stair between the carriage floor and the ground. He held a hand out to me.

"My lady knight, we have arrived! Would you like assistance getting out of the carriage?"

My jaw dropped in shock.

"What? Is there something on my face?"

Blinking rapidly, I pulled my face into a less shocked expression.

"No, no. Your face is perfect. Um, perfectly fine, I mean."

I couldn't believe that come out of my mouth. Well, now there was no hiding the flush on my face, so I might as well roll with it.

"I don't think anyone has ever offered me their assistance getting out of the carriage before."

"Really? Not ever? Is it offensive?"

His brow furrowed in worry. I couldn't help but laugh.

"It's not offensive at all," I told him and placed my hand in his still outstretched one. "In fact, it's rather lovely."

He squeezed my hand and stepped to the side so that I could get out of the carriage. I shivered slightly at his touch. Hopefully he would mistake it for shivering from the change of temperature from the warm carriage to the early spring streets, and not realize it was from desire.

You know, it wouldn't be so bad if he did know you were shivering at the mere touch of his hand, a voice that sounded suspiciously like my mother's said in the back of my mind. I shook the thought away and allowed him to help me out of the carriage.

I found myself standing on a street that I recognized as the outskirts of the Merchant's District, surrounded on all sides by carts whose owners hawked items of all shapes and sizes for sale. Their voices blended together into a harmonic cacophony that reminded me of the practice fields. The farther into the district you got, the shops changed from carts to stalls to full stone buildings and the less shouting you heard. The prices also got higher, but that usually wasn't a problem for me. I could see carts stacked with potions, cloth, and several varieties of baked goods. The one salesman I didn't see or hear was a bookseller.

Turning to where Avery stood beside me, I realized he had never released my hand. It just felt right somehow. Raising an eyebrow quizzically, I glanced down at our intertwined hands and back up at his smiling face.

"Where do we start?"

* * *

AVERY

It was totally inappropriate for me to still be holding Genevieve's hands more than ten minutes after we'd gotten out of the carriage, but I didn't want to let go. I blushed and released her hand, knowing that we'd be recognized if we weren't careful.

I held out my elbow for her to give her someplace more acceptable to place her hand. She took it with a small smile and the warmth that spread over me was like a beam of sunlight shone directly at me.

"The stall I saw was right around the corner, if you don't mind a bit of a walk, my lady?"

We wandered through the marketplace, stopping occasionally to look at something displayed in a window or to taste something freshly cooked. I loved it. As we rounded the corner, I could see the shop that I'd wanted to visit, and the shopkeeper standing out in front of it. I caught the shopkeeper's eye and his smile widened, showing teeth that were slightly crooked. When we got closer, he spoke.

"Welcome, fair friends! My name is Bartholomew, and this is my selection of books! Please let me know if there's anything in particular my assistant, James, or I can help you with while you search. Please refer to me with he pronouns, and to James with xie pronouns."

He waved towards his assistant, a tall, willowy person with grey hair who looked as though xie might blow away in any strong gust. I nodded my understanding and saw Genevieve do the same.

"Our books are shelved by genre, then by author name, and then alphabetically by title. If there's something you cannot find, we may be able to procure it for you from one of our contacts throughout the city. We're fairly well connected between the two of us."

He finally took a breath of the cold winter air and smiled at the pair of us.

"That's the whole spiel I've got for you. Enjoy your perusals!"

We exchanged an amused glance and grabbed a basket each, entering the labyrinth of carts with determination. I could still hear the wind whistling through the slats of the carts surrounding us but the cold didn't reach my skin, which I was grateful for. Genevieve's shoulders relaxed under her wool coat as she came into the shelter of the labyrinth.

The drafts off of the nearby ocean were always harsh and bitter, even in warmer parts of the year. But between the shelves, it felt warm enough to remove the thick knitted gloves I'd needed in the streets.

I hadn't had any particular books in mind when he recommended stopping by the stall, but the task of finding a perfect gift for Alys had my brain working hard. I would never admit this, but I had no gift for Alys, either.

Several of her classmates had sworn off giving her gifts entirely, even if they were interested in pursuing a relationship with her. I knew her better than most people did, but I was fairly certain that I've only been successful in getting her a gift she actually wanted twice in the decade that I'd been her mentor and friend. If we were lucky, both of us could find something that would impress the famously finicky woman that we both knew and loved.

Unfortunately, I had absolutely no idea what to buy her for her birthday. I whirled around, allowing my cloak to twirl around me in a flourish. Genevieve laughed, a flush creeping across her round cheeks.

"So, have you got any ideas for what to get Alys?"

Genevieve hesitated, shifting her weight from foot to foot before answering.

"She mentioned wanting to learn about the history of Teagan and the region, since her regional education was lacking at the Academy... I was hoping to do something like that."

"Well, you picked the right shopping companion, then. I happen to be an expert on our duchies' shared history. But which would be best for Alys?"

I tapped a finger on my slightly scruffy chin in thought, going through the many histories I'd read of the region. Some were too loose with their actual history, others glossed over the realities of the region's struggles and others were just poorly written. I didn't want Genevieve to take any of those home for her sister. Just like that, I knew exactly what to get her. I clapped my hands together lightly and stepped closer to my companion.

"I believe there was a multi-volume set printed a few years ago that was incredibly thorough. Off to the history section we go!"

I held out my hand to her and she took it without a second's hesitation. Someone else might have blamed the spark on the fact that we were bundled in wool, but I knew better. I ran a bare finger along the books on the cart as I searched for the section I wanted, clucking my tongue lightly as I made note of books I wanted to look at later. I couldn't allow myself to be distracted so easily or Genevieve would think I had forgotten our purpose. I could feel her eyes on me as I searched, and heard her turn and look in the carts opposite me after a moment.

"Let me know if you find it first," she told me. "I'll call you if I do."

I rounded the cover and spotted the tooled leather cover that I was looking for among a very wide selection of books that my hands itched to get ahold of. I called out to her and waited next to them, perusing the other titles in the section. It was rare for me to buy books for myself that were not magic-related since I had easy access to both the Academy's library and my mother's, but I always kept an eye out for texts that would fit well in her collection.

Father had never been particularly interested in the contents of the library, but Mother had made expanding it her life's work. Wolvington was her home duchy, and she had insisted on bringing me up there, rather than the palace that was also my birthright. I had grown up to love the rolling hills and forests as much as she did, and to have a strong sense of responsibility for everyone who resided within our townships. Safety and an education were the most important things that I could give the people that relied on me, and you couldn't have true education without a library.

"Now, we'll want to avoid any translations by Williams or Bossuet, because they're terrible on several levels," I informed her. "Starting with the fact that they completely ignore the realities of life in our duchies for those who aren't nobles."

Genevieve guffawed. The bright sound echoed off the carts around the two of us. She laughed so loudly and freely that a snort escaped from behind the hand she used to cover her mouth and nose, and I was transfixed. I never would've heard anything similar from her younger sister, who tended to be prim and proper at all costs.

After the sound escaped her, a small wrinkle formed between her eyebrows, but a grin from me had it smoothing out just as quickly. I thought I spotted a single dimple on her right cheek and knew that I would do almost anything to see it again. She doubled over in laughter that I couldn't resist joining her in.

"Well that was a thing that happened," she said once she regained her composure. She wiped drops of water from her eyes. "That was just so unexpected, especially from a scholar and a duke. Those two are big names from what I remember from my studies."

"Yeah, and they're awful human beings. Have you met them?"

The wrinkle reappeared between her eyebrows as she stared at me. When she spoke, her voice was an octave higher than normal, and slightly breathy.

"Met them? Why would I have met two of the most well-known historians in Elisade?"

Oh. Right. As a knight, she would have more important things to do than waste time in King Bayard's councils.

"I forgot that you wouldn't have met historians so easily as I would have, not being a politician or a scholar," I admitted. She raised her eyebrows at me, a smile wide on her face. I caught an uninterrupted glimpse of the dimple on her right cheek. It made my heart ache.

"No, no I'm not. I'm not quite as important as all that in the grand scheme of Elisadean politics. I'm much better at the hacking and slashing in general."

"And I'm sure you're wonderful at it, to be on my nephew's honor guard as a first year knight."

She ducked her head.

"I'm all right, I guess," she mumbled. She turned her attention to the shelf of tomes in front of them. "So, what do you think of Welton and Pina?"

"Oh, they're delightful people. Their histories tend to be pretty inclusive, too, though they tend to be more accurate the further north you go. I'd love to see if they have Brusseau's collection..."

My eyes glanced over the names on the shelf, from Baxter to Quexada to Valencia, until finally I found what I was looking for.

Grabbing the first volume of the set from the shelf, I brandished it at Genevieve like a dagger.

"Did you know that my mother tried to set me up with Ursula the last time she came to the library at Wolvington?"

She stiffened, then smirked at me. The sunlight from above the carts caught the twinkle in her eye. She was beautiful.

"What, is she a troll or something? Your life must be terrible, being set up with all these women."

I laughed loudly.

"They aren't all bad, but I have been on more than my share of dates since my first season. Ursula has a true adoration for the female form, and not into anyone romantically, so I wasn't quite her type. But we did have a lovely time at the opera together."

"I see. And how does that affect her history telling skills?"

"Oh it doesn't. It's just one of my favorite stories to surprise people with. The third and fourth volume are those that apply most to Teagan and Wolvington, but the full set is really worth buying."

I turned the book over and nearly choked on the gasp that burst from my chest at the number.

"Well, maybe. How much do you *actually* like your sister?"

Genevieve laughed, and it felt like my heart was trying to take flight from my chest to join the sound. I couldn't remember ever enjoying an afternoon with a new person so entirely, and I didn't want it to end.

GENEVIEVE

I nearly floated out of the carriage later that evening when it arrived at my home. I didn't even care about the interrogation that was inevitable as soon as I stepped through the doors.

It had been such a good afternoon. We both kept losing track of time, and I had bought many more books than I had originally intended. In my defense, so had Avery.

"Did he seem to be interested in you as a romantic partner?" Mama demanded before I'd even hung up my coat.

"Well, I think it's a little early for that, don't you?" I asked, looking to Alys for help. Taking my cue, she stepped into the discussion and allowed me to take off my outerwear.

"I don't think that he would have invited her to go shopping with him if he hadn't been interested in her romantically. Not without telling her, anyway."

It warmed my heart to hear Alys say that. Despite my previously unrequited crush on him, I didn't know him all that well. Hopefully, I could fix that soon.

"I suppose that you are right. He has never been one to lead anyone on from all the gossip I've heard..." Mama tapped a finger on her nose then nodded. "Well, we'll just have to find new ways to push you two together. I will find out which galas he is scheduled to attend for the rest of the month and which ones we can make work for your schedule."

I groaned. I knew what that meant. I was going to need more fashionable gowns than what I had, if I was to make a good impression on the court in my role as heir to Teagan as well as a knight. I would soon be headed back to the Merchant's District, probably with my mother and sister in tow. My much more fashionable family members would certainly find me something beautiful to wear. I could only hope that I would still be able to walk in whatever they decided to put me in.

6

POPPY

I couldn't keep myself from fidgeting with the flat, rounded collar of my gown with my free hand. My other arm was held straight out in front of me with the heavy gown encased in a burlap sack that would protect it from any road dust we'd encountered on the carriage ride over.

"That has to be heavy holding the dress like that. You're going to put your arm to sleep, love. Let me hold it for you."

I blushed at the sound of him calling me "love" but pulled the dress away from him.

"Are you saying I can't hold this gown up? It's a dress, it isn't that heavy, Cormac."

He rolled his eyes.

"Sure, and if it was a normal dress I would never question your strength. But that dress right there weighs more than a good suit of leather armor, and it's taller than you are. I'm just saying that I would be willing to hold onto it while we wait for Ser Genevieve to come fetch us."

I thought about it before realizing that he was right. I offered him my arm and he took the gown gently.

"You drop it and you die, blacksmith," I reminded him ominously. "I don't care how cute you think you are."

He grinned at me. Carefully, he lifted the gown over his left shoulder, holding the hanger with three fingers. It fell against his back and nearly knocked the wind out of him.

"I underestimated how heavy this would be, even knowing what it's made out of," he said with a grimace.

"I'm not taking it back!" I laughed. "You offered your big strong man arms, so now you get to put them to use."

He chuckled and nodded. We fell into a companionable silence, letting the sounds of the hustle and bustle that came from the servant's entrance wash over us. I hadn't been at the palace since I was very young, and it was a very different experience being back at the servant's quarters. As if sensing I needed a distraction, Cormac asked me a question.

"Is this your first time visiting the palace?"

That was not exactly a distraction. A harsh laugh escaped my mouth while I shook my head. It didn't sound like me, but I didn't want to hide this from Cormac.

"I used to live here as a child alongside my mother, but I haven't been back since she passed."

He raised both eyebrows at me in shock.

"You lived in the palace? How did I not know that?"

"I didn't really want anybody to know. Ma was a maid for Queen Amelie before..." I allowed the sentence to trail off, and Cormac understood.

I only nodded. Queen Amelia had been murdered, and through the investigation, it had been revealed that a servant had delivered the fatal poison, though the country eventually learned it was sent from Linbourne. Her bevy of servants had been dismissed, as they were no longer needed.

"She couldn't work as a lady's maid after that, so she took up work as a seamstress. I could never bring myself to come back, till now."

"I didn't realize. I wouldn't have made you come back if I'd known, Poppy. Are you sure you're all right with being here? I can take care of the delivery."

I smiled up at him through watery eyes. The guilt was plain on his handsome face.

"You cannot take care of the delivery. If there are any alterations to be made, you do not know how to make them in the silk without destroying it, and you know it. But I dearly appreciate the offer. Don't worry, dear. If it had been a problem, I would have asked Genevieve to come pick up the dress instead. We all have to face our fears sometime. I'm nearly fifty years old. It's time to face this one, now that I have an opportunity."

His gaze was fixed on my face, searching for something. I could only guess that he found it.

"I suppose. But if you're uncomfortable, you can always leave. I'll make an excuse for you."

He smiled tentatively at me and I bumped my shoulder against his elbow. He bumped me back gently.

"You two waiting for Ser Genevieve?"

A servant stood in the doorway, watching us expectantly. His arms were crossed over Teagan-colored livery. We both nodded.

"Well, come along then. Can't keep the knight waiting all day, now can we?"

The servant didn't wait for a response before turning and walking away. Cormac passed me an amused glance.

"It's your time to shine, love. You go first."

I took a deep breath before taking my first steps into the castle for the first time in more than thirty years. Cormac waited for a moment, then followed after me.

GENEVIEVE

A knock sounded on the door, echoing through the medium sized dressing room that mother and I were waiting in.

"Come in!" I called.

It opened to reveal the people we were waiting for, guided by Juniper. The craftspeople were dressed so sharply they would have fit in among the nobles they were there to dress. Poppy and Cormac filed in and looked around the room.

Noticing Mama, Cormac bent at the waist in as deep a bow he could manage in the crowded room. She nodded at him, then gestured for him to rise.

"We're not standing on ceremony here. I cannot wait to see this creation!"

She stepped out of their way so they could get to the center of the room, where a tailor's pedestal was set up.

"Well, are you pleased with the results?" I asked the team that stood before me.

They both answered with huge grins and sparkling eyes. This was a good sign.

"Well let's see it then!" Mama implored.

Cormac turned and presented the burlap bag to Poppy. Without further ado, they unfolded the burlap from the hanger and let it drop to the floor.

"Oh, it's a masterpiece," I gasped. I heard Mother mutter something that sounded positive to each other.

Cormac excused himself to wait in the hall while the tailor helped me get into the gown. It wouldn't be appropriate for a man to be in the room for that. As soon as Poppy had stepped away, I spun a tight circle. The layers of silk and chainmail blossomed around me like a deadly blue and bronze rose. I watched everything in the mirror. I didn't want to take my eyes off of myself, but had to glance at Poppy, who had kneeled down next to me and was placing pins in the back of the gown.

"It would have been absolutely stunning with a corset in it," the Duchess said wistfully.

"It may have been stunning, but it would have left me stunned if I'd had to fight in it," I reminded my mother airily. "Besides, it doesn't need it. The chainmail does exactly what a corset does, and it's not like anyone will notice the lack thereof."

"I suppose," she sighed dramatically. "It really is beautifully crafted, my dear. You chose your tailor well."

"Thank you, Mama. I'm glad to hear you approve," I replied, turning my head away so that Mama wouldn't see me roll my eyes. It didn't work.

"Tut tut! A lady does not roll her eyes."

"Then I guess it's a good thing I'm a knight and a lady - and knights definitely roll their eyes."

I turned at Poppy's gentle urging while they worked, just in time to see Mama roll her eyes.

"Aha!" I crowed. "Now who isn't acting like a lady, Mama?"

She smiled impishly back at me, a glint in her hazel eyes.

"A lady gets to have a little fun every once in a while."

I could hear Poppy trying to stifle a giggle while they worked. I didn't bother to hide my own laughter.

"Duchess Vivienne, would it be okay if we brought Cormac in? I need him to take out a few links in the bottom so that I can make it fit properly."

"Oh, that isn't a problem. Let's get Genevieve into something else so you can work on that gown more quickly."

Poppy nodded, and the Duchess leapt gracefully from her

chair, holding up the simple dressing gown that I had taken off in the first place. Poppy lowered the chainmail gown to my ankles, allowing me to step out of it without issue.

Mama helped me into my gown, then brushed wisps of my brown hair away from my eyes with a soft smile.

Poppy allowed the gown to rest on the floor, straightening their back with a series of pops that had Genevieve grimacing.

"Not to be worried, miss. It happens when you spend your life bent over around other people's behinds." Poppy grinned.

Mama let out a giggle that turned into a snort at the tailor's frankness.

"Poppy, I like you," she declared. "No matter how this turns out, we'll definitely be visiting you more often when my family is in town."

"I look forward to seeing you, my lady." Poppy curtsied politely. "Would it be all right for Cormac to come in now?"

The duchess waved a hand, realizing she'd gone off topic when they were in a time crunch.

"Oh, of course, of course. We're all appropriately clothed now."

Raising their voice, the tailor called the blacksmith in. Cormac had to duck his head to enter the arched doorway without bashing it.

Poppy and I welcomed him with smiles.

"Now, Cormac, it's been years since I saw you! I won't take up much of your time, but I would love to visit your forge and catch up once this is done. I've got to run and see to everything else for our other children, but I'm so glad you were able to help my Genevieve with this little project of hers."

I stiffened at having this called a "little project" but Mama didn't notice.

She swanned out of the room in a cloud of silk and taffeta, leaving the three of us alone together.

"I'd forgotten how strong a presence milady was," Cormac said. He wiped the back of his hand across his brow to mime wiping sweat off. Poppy laughed.

"Come on now, we haven't got all day to get this done."

"You sort of do, actually?" I told them. "I only have to show the Knight Commander and get his approval before the ball, which isn't until next week."

"Aye, but that doesn't mean we're going to use all that time for alterations. These are minor. We can, and we will, fix it now."

Poppy was so determined that I didn't dare argue with them. They both declined an offer of refreshments, but I had nowhere to be, so I settled into the chair in the corner of the room with my book. There was no point getting in their way, at least until Alys arrived.

At the very least, I would be able to hear Alys's opinionated thoughts on the gown before it debuted. My thought process was that I'd rather be nervous and upset about whatever remarks may come out of my sister's mouth now, than on the night of the ball. That was a lesson I learned the hard way.

Alys and I might currently have a truce when it came to barbed comments and backhanded compliments, but that wasn't guaranteed to last.

After almost an hour, I thought that Poppy and Cormac looked to be almost done with their alterations. They were working together to put the dress back together the right way when Alys swept through the door.

I have no idea how she always managed to enter a room at the best possible time, but it was one of the skills that I had always admired about my sister.

Alys was wearing a beautiful plush crimson gown today, with a ridiculously wide train that barely fit through the door behind her. I had to admit that it looked wonderful on her, fitting tightly to her ample curves in a way that still looked comfortable. I couldn't help but feel a twinge of jealousy, knowing that I would never look that good in the same gown.

A similar look of jealousy crossed Alys's face when she looked at the chainmail gown on the mannequin. Her eyes widened so far that I worried they'd fall out of her head.

"Oh my god, this is the most beautiful dress I've ever seen," Alys squealed. "This is just stunning, Gen!"

I couldn't stop a grin from spreading across my face.

"You should see it on her," Poppy chimed in. "She makes it work even better than I imagined it."

Alys kept circling Poppy and Cormac as they worked, seeing the gown from all the possible angles.

"Oh, it's lovely. Just wait until Avery sees you in it!"

"Avery, eh? Have you got a beau, Genevieve?" Cormac asked around a mouthful of chain links. Poppy had gone quiet, apparently focusing on the work in their hands. Alys looked taken aback at the familiar tone that Cormac used with me and downright shocked when I laughed.

"He's hardly a beau, you old gossip. He's the King's son, and that doesn't leave this room."

"Aye, aye. Would ye like him to be your beau, though? That's an ambitious match, even for the heiress of the house of Teagan."

"And yet, it's a perfect one. Duke Avery's a wonderful man," Alys said. "Plus, he and Genevieve would make such a great pair!"

"I don't believe I've met the Duke..." the blacksmith mused. "How about you, Pop?"

"I've never had the pleasure," Poppy said formally, diving back into the seam they were taking in on the bodice.

I caught Cormac's eye, confused by their sudden distance from the conversation. He shook his head and changed the subject.

"What brings you to this fitting, Lady Alys? I wasn't expecting to see you today."

At that comment, Alys took a closer look at the blacksmith sitting on the floor.

"You remember Cormac, don't you, Alys? From Teagan?" I prompted. Recognition lit her face up.

"Ah, of course!" she declared. "I didn't even recognize you! Not that I was expecting to see you, of course."

I grinned at the two of them.

"Surprise!"

"What were you expecting, if not me, my lady?" Cormac asked with a gentlemanly smile.

"I was expecting to just find our fabulous tailor finishing up the gown after the final fitting."

That was my cue.

"Alys has a request for you, Poppy."

Poppy looked up, joining the conversation intentionally for the first time since Alys had arrived. They took the spare needle out from between their teeth, stashed it in the fold of their sleeve and smiled genuinely.

"How can I help you, dearie?"

Alys turned shy suddenly, staring intently at the floor where she was grinding the toe of her slipper. I rolled my eyes, which of course Alys saw. With a deep breath, the words tumbled out.

"Um, I was hoping... wondering really, if you had any time to take on an additional gown for the ball?"

Poppy raised their thick eyebrows at the request.

"Left it a bit late, haven't you?"

Alys's face turned pink, and she nodded, still not meeting Poppy's gaze.

"Let me finish up your sister's gown, and then we can sit and see what I can do for you," Poppy said. "It shouldn't be more than half an hour before we're done here. Right Cormac?"

The blacksmith nodded, continuing with his work. I cleared a spot on the couch for my sister, sliding my bare feet under her behind where she sat.

Alys slid onto the open-sided couch much more gracefully than her query had been, looked at me and stuck out her tongue. The childlike gesture drew a laugh from both of the craftspeople on the floor, and a smile from me. Gesturing to the messy stack of books beside her, I silently offered them to her. She peered at the stack and pulled one from the middle. After all these years, I was almost convinced that part of Alys's magic was keeping everything balanced, because the books did not collapse onto one another like I was sure they would have if I'd tried.

The room fell into companionable silence, the four of us each at our own tasks. The quiet was only broken by Poppy humming lightly to themself, and Cormac getting their attention to hand them the pieces of mail as he finished them.

The tailor rose from the floor slowly after a while, circling the gown repeatedly where it hung on the mannequin. I got a little dizzy watching them before they clapped their hands together.

"Yes, I think this will do nicely. Ser, I've left it a chain looser than I normally would have, which ought to give you a little more freedom of movement. Would you like to try it on one more time before I tend to the Lady?"

"Oh heavens no. I trust the changes you've made here, and I wouldn't want to take up any more of your day. You've been here for ages!"

Poppy nodded with a pleased smile. Alys took advantage of this to slide between us, brandishing a rough-edged piece of paper at the tailor.

"The gown I'd like to commission is not a particularly difficult one, if you'd like to take a look?"

I took that as my cue to leave and began unlacing the back of the gown from the mannequin. I jumped when Cormac knelt next to me, lifting the gown from the bottom.

"Let me help you carry this, Genevieve. It's quite unwieldy when it's not on a frame."

"You know I can handle it, Cormac. I could lift you if I needed to."

"Aye, you could try!" He laughed. Neither Poppy nor Alys spared us a glance.

"You're welcome to accompany me, at any rate. I'd be glad for the company."

He smiled gently, and gestured for me to lift the gown from where he had it bunched at the mannequin's waist. I did so, fixing my grasp so that I could lift the extremely heavy garment without injuring myself. I placed my arms over his, allowing him to pull away, but he didn't. Instead, he kept his hands at the ready in case I dropped it.

Behind us, I could hear Alys and Poppy talking animatedly and quietly about the gown she wanted.

"Would you care to assist me, Cormac? I'll need help getting the doors opened with this in my hands as I make my way to the Knight Commander's office."

He stepped around me to do just that.

"With pleasure, my lady."

* * *

AVERY

I had finally settled into a peaceful spot in the back corner of the palace library, ensconced in a plush armchair with a novel in my hand. Everything was perfect, until a tentative voice broke into the near silence.

"Excuse me, Duke Avery?"

I looked up to see a servant dressed in the simple black and white palace uniform looking down at me. Bright blue eyes looked at me from under nearly white blonde fringe with a polite smile on their lips. Their hair was tied back with a mulberry ribbon that made me think of Genevieve.

"Yes, how can I help you...?" I waited for them to tell me their name. They didn't take the bait.

"I was sent to ask you to come to Knight Commander Cedric's office at your earliest convenience."

I snapped my book closed with a sigh. The remainder of this novel would have to wait for later.

"I suppose now is as convenient as any other time. Thank you for coming to fetch me. I appreciate it."

They dipped into a bow and walked away. Pulling myself up from the chair, I wondered what could have cousin Cedric summoning me right now. He had taught me to fight many years ago, but with less than two weeks till the ball and with a bevy of pages and squires under his command, he had to have his hands full. Nevertheless, I made my way out of the library and up the two flights of stairs that would bring me to his office. I crossed paths with several of the older knights, though they didn't acknowledge me, and several servants I recognized from the kitchens.

Knocking lightly on the door, I didn't wait to enter. I immediately regretted that choice. A familiar form twirled in a gown that looked to be made of a combination of silk, leather and ...chainmail?

"Duke Avery! What are you doing here?"

The shock was clear on her face, which was almost the same deep blue color as her gown by now. I knew my cheeks would be a similar color. She was stunning. I turned around quickly, trying to hide the blush on my face. Genevieve and I hadn't seen each other since I'd returned from Wolvington.

"Oh my gods, I'm so sorry Ser Genevieve," I spluttered. "I'm sorry, Knight Commander. I didn't realize you were busy."

Knight Commander Cedric looked confused.

"Come in boy, it's not like she's naked in here. Now why are you here?"

"One of the servants mentioned that you wanted to see me?"

Cedric's look of confusion deepened, making the wrinkles in his face look permanently carved into his stone-like face.

"I have no idea what you're talking about, my good Duke. Do you know the servant?"

I felt my face pucker in confusion, matching my cousins much older expression. Genevieve's face reddened even more, but I had no idea why.

"I vaguely recognized them, but I couldn't tell you a name. They were about yay high, very pale with white blonde hair and wearing a palace uniform?" I gestured to my shoulder.

Genevieve's expression clouded, her face growing stormier by the minute.

"Were they wearing a mulberry ribbon in their hair?"

"Why, yes, they were!" I cried, happy that someone knew who I was talking about. She covered her face with her tan, callused hands.

"I suspect that would be my maidservant Juniper, sirs. They have quite the mind of their own," her voice trailed off.

"Juniper, you say? Well, that would explain it," Cedric said, his voice gravelly with amusement. Petra had been rather famous for her pranks before Genevieve had hired her away. "I see that she hasn't lost her touch since she left the palace."

"No, ser," Genevieve said, laughing nervously before regaining a little bit of confidence. "Nor would I want them to."

"Indeed."

I was still confused, but I felt like my face was a normal color again, which was a relief.

"Right, so does anyone know why I'm here, exactly?" I asked.

"Well, I was about to duel with our knight here, to test out this... something of a dress for the prince's ball. But since you're here, would you like to do the honors?"

My mouth fell open. Glancing at Genevieve, I saw her expression mirrored my own.

"Knight Commander, I am hardly a warrior of Ser Genevieve's caliber," I protested. "I'm hardly qualified-"

Cedric silenced me with a wave of his hand.

"Nonsense, my boy. You are perfectly capable of helping her with this test. I would know! I trained you myself, did I not?"

That was true, but I still hesitated. I didn't want to make a fool of myself, which was sure to happen if I dueled Genevieve. Glancing at Cedric's determined expression, I took a deep breath and squared my shoulders.

"I'll do whatever you require, my lord, as long as it is acceptable to our knight."

Genevieve snapped her mouth shut as both Cedric and I turned to her where she stood in the center of the room. A blush flooded across her face again, spreading through what I could see of her chest.

"What weapons shall we use, then?" she asked.

"How about the short swords?" the Knight Commander mused. "Those are more useful in close combat like you're likely to find if someone comes after Prince Julian."

He whirled to me, looked me up and down and nodded.

"Well, that's settled then," Cedric said with a cheerful clap. "Let's get you suited up, my boy! We'll meet you at the practice grounds in half an hour, shall we?"

"Yes, ser." I bowed to the Knight Commander and repeated the motion to Genevieve. Without speaking further, I walked out of the Knight Commander's study. Pausing to pull myself together, I was surprised to hear the two knights speak again.

"Well, this ought to be a good way for you two to get to know each other, now won't it?"

There was a note of amusement in the older man's voice. I

pressed my ear to the door, wanting to hear more. Genevieve spluttered and Cedric laughed.

"What are you talking about?" she asked the man who had been in charge of her training for over a decade.

"What, did you think that I was actually surprised by Juniper sending in the lord Duke? Come now, my girl. My acting skills aren't that good."

It was then that I realized that I had been played.

"Oh my gods," I muttered. "I'm going to get my royal behind kicked just to get to know a pretty lady, aren't I?"

That was exactly what would happen, but I didn't regret the opportunity one bit.

* * *

GENEVIEVE

I could not believe Juniper's nerve. And yet, I was more surprised that my mother had gotten the Knight Commander involved in the scheme to force us together at every opportunity. He'd arrived back in the capital only yesterday.

Now I stood in my ball gown in the red brown dirt of the training ring in the castle courtyard, shifting my weight from foot to foot as I got used to the weight of it on my body.

Avery leaped over the simple wooden fence with ease, having changed into a simple long-sleeved linen tunic and trousers. He walked as if he belonged in the ring as much as I did. A servant I didn't recognize handed him a simple leather vest that would protect him from any body blows I managed to land on him during the duel. He shrugged it on and the servant handed him a pair of palace issue rapiers. I hoped that that was a good sign. As he'd said, he wasn't as practiced a warrior as I am, no matter how well Knight Commander Cedric had trained him. And I knew that he would be trained well if Cedric had been in charge of him, even if he did prefer to spend his days working in the library or using his glamour magic to help heal warriors. This meant that he was likely to be out of practice - something that I was not.

I watched his glance sweep around the ring, checking for hills and valleys in the packed dirt beneath our feet, or weak points in the fence that encircled us. He wouldn't find anything, I knew. I had done the same check on my arrival.

"Are you prepared for battle?"

Knight Commander Cedric's voice rang out. We both turned to where he perched on the sturdy, waist-height wooden fence. It was a familiar sight to all in the palace who had seen him cast his eagle eyes over the pages and squires in his care.

Avery grinned at the man, showing off his gleaming smile, before turning back to me. I couldn't help but hope that the feelings that were burgeoning in my chest wouldn't cause me to lose the ability to fight in the gown I already loved. Pages, squires and my fellow knights had gathered around the outside of the fence. I spotted my friend and former knight master Ser Raoul in the crowd, and knew that they would be taking bets on who would win. I only hoped I wouldn't disappoint them, and myself. A deep breath worked to steady me.

"Ready, Knight Commander!" I called, raising my right hand and sword.

Avery raised his left hand and blade to echo my call. I was intrigued to note that that his left hand was his dominant hand, filing it away for reference later, and stepped toward the dueling lines.

"Take your places! This'll be a clean fight, with wrapped swords."

Two of the squires hopped over the fence with lengths of linen that would be perfect to ensure there were no unsightly gashes made during this duel. They would not, however, make the strike of the blades any less powerful. I didn't recognize either of the squires, but Avery thanked the one helping him with a kind smile that made my heart flutter. He really was one of the most handsome men I'd ever seen. The fact that he was kind to everyone he came into contact with only enhanced my attraction to him. Without saying a word to each other, we wrapped our blades and got into position. The dueling lines were marked with flat stones carved deeply into the packed dirt floor of the ring with about a foot of space between them.

"Are you sure you want to do this?" I asked, too low for any of the others around us to hear. The bystanders were chattering around the edges of the fence, waiting for the duel to start. Avery offered me a crooked smile and a small shrug that made my pulse race.

"I do as my Knight Commander commands. Plus, we can all use the exercise, can't we?"

"I suppose so," I said dubiously. "Are you ready?"

He squared his shoulders.

"Ready as I'll ever be!"

"This is an exhibition, so show off your skills, you two. First one to strike flesh or to knock the other's blade to the ground wins. Let the duel commence!" Knight Commander Cedric punctuated the roar with an ear-piercing whistle.

We began to circle each other in the ring, getting a feel for the other's movements and body language. We were relatively evenly matched, as far as our physical builds went. They were similar heights, though I suspected that I was more muscular. I allowed my gaze to linger for just a moment on the way his biceps bulged with his grip on the rapiers. Pulling my gaze back to his weapons, his first thrust came from the right.

I parried it deftly from the left, moving quickly and attempting a low strike from my right. He deflected it and we pulled away from each other, continuing our circling. He was faster than I had expected. We were both soon working to catch our breath and sight of our opponents. The cold wind swirled the dirt around us, whipping my skirts up. I was grateful for the trousers that Poppy had built into the dress at that moment, otherwise my legs would have been lashed by the dirt.

I leapt towards him and he caught my strike with the leather and wood hilt of his left rapier. He pushed me away with the blade of his other sword.

"You're pretty good at this," I said, chest heaving.

"I'm very good at this," he corrected. "Didn't you know I've been in countless duels while in school?"

"No, I did not."

I lunged again and he barely got his rapier up before my blade crashed into his chest and face. It would have been a tragedy to put a black eye on his beautiful face.

"Who was foolish enough to duel the king's son?"

He backed up, shaking his arm from the impact of the blow I'd nearly landed.

"Well, I had a very short temper, and there were tons of little lordlings wishing to prove they were better than the spare prince. I got good fast."

He spotted his chance to strike right as he finished speaking. Avery came after me with a flurry of blows that I was barely able to block. My swords were engaged with his, but I saw an opening for some ingenuity. I lifted an elbow and hammered it towards his forehead. He lifted his sword to stop me and accidentally struck himself with it. I used the opportunity to land a blow with the flat of my blade on his ribs.

He stumbled and began to crumple. He had the presence of mind to fling his blades to the side so he wouldn't fall on them. I dropped my own blades into the dirt without a second thought. Spreading the petals of my skirt out, I rushed to catch him.

"We have a winner!" Cedric roared as my knees hit the ground, arms wrapped around Avery's waist.

I lowered him to the dirt as gently as I could, resting his head on my thighs. I knew he'd lose consciousness soon if we weren't careful, just based on the blows that had landed.

"I've got you," I whispered. "I'm here. I've got you."

I lifted my head, and yelled to the squires.

"We're gonna need a healer!"

I heard Avery speaking very softly, and leaned down as much as I could with the chainmail bodice.

"Yes, my lord?"

He took a deep breath and fluttered his eyes like he wanted to open them.

"You're real pretty, Genevieve."

I hoped that anyone looking at me would attribute the blush that spread over my cheeks and neck to the battle I had just finished. A healer arrived at the ring a moment later, relieving me of my charge. They relaxed once they made physical contact with Avery which made me feel whole lot better.

"He'll be fine. Give him a few hours and he'll be back to normal," they reassured me. Several other healers joined the first, lifting Avery from the ground.

"We'll take him to the hospital wing and keep an eye on him."

I nodded and stood, dusting the dirt as best as I could from my skirt. It didn't do much. The red dirt had made its home in the silk. Poppy was going to kill me.

CORMAC

It was finally time to have the dinner Poppy and I had agreed on. I had the perfect place chosen and asked a friend who worked there to hold a table near the window for us. Everything was going perfect, so far.

I'd slicked my hair and beard into shape with a bit of potion I'd found in the marketplace. It smelled like elderberries, which was soothing. Between that and the plum tailored jacket that I wanted to surprise Poppy with, I was feeling quite handsome.

That didn't keep my thoughts from racing, from wondering if I wasn't going to screw up the best friendship I'd ever had on the chance that we could make this relationship even more, somehow. I was so nervous I wanted to vomit, but I couldn't do that without damaging the clothing I'd bought just for the occasion.

I so desperately wanted tonight to go well. We'd been kissing and flirting more in the last week or so, which had been wonderful. I had enjoyed every minute of it, just the way I had our friendship over the last decade. Sometimes I caught Poppy's gaze and wondered if maybe they didn't want to go further, but I hadn't wanted to push them before they were sure.

Not until after this dinner, anyway. After this, we were going to need to have a conversation about how we wanted to proceed. That was what had me nervous, more than anything. I desperately didn't want to lose them as a friend, no matter what. This dinner would not be the end of our friendship. In my heart of hearts, I knew that. I had to focus on what it could turn into instead.

I smoothed my hands down the plush fabric of my jacket and took a few deep breaths. Before I could psych myself out again, I walked out the door, locking the forge for the night, and whispered a silent prayer to the Goddess for luck.

POPPY

Cormac and I decided to take the long way home from the restaurant he'd taken us to. Our dinner had been wonderful, once I'd gotten past the awkwardness I felt. The food had been exquisite and his company was wonderful, as always.

He offered me his arm and I took it, relishing the closeness that it brought to us. The air around us was cool but the heat that passed between our bodies made it comfortable.

Flowers were starting to pop up all in the small raised beds that were set in front of the other shops we walked past on our way back to the apartment I lived in above my shop. We took turns pointing out different plants that we liked as we walked. He tended to like the simpler shrubbery and small trees while I liked the more delicate plants with stems and leaves that looked like lacework. It seemed appropriate somehow, given our different professions.

I was looking forward to a nice hot drink and snuggling up with Cormac when we got home. It would be the perfect end to a perfect day.

When we arrived at the shop, however, I stopped short at the sight of Cormac's apprentice sitting on the stoop with the gown that we had delivered earlier that day spread across his lap. I didn't need him to explain what happened when I saw red brown over the beautiful blue silk.

"I knew this was going to happen," I scoffed, throwing my hands in the air. "It's the middle of winter! Why couldn't they duel inside where they wouldn't get dirt on everything?"

I unlocked the door and stalked to the back of the shop to reset the mannequin so I could work on this dress again. Finn followed after me as quickly as he could while still carrying the dress. He was young and strong, but I knew the dress was unwieldy to carry.

"I'm going to have to replace all of the silk panels on the front of the gown," I groused. "All of them! Oh, I'm going to charge her extra for this."

By the time Cormac and Finn actually made it back to the workshop, my voice had dropped to a much more reasonable growl. Cormac helped him to slide the dress over the top of the mannequin and we all breathed a sigh of relief. As soon as his hands were free, Finn started digging through his pockets.

"She sent a coin purse with me, Poppy, and her apologies. She swears she'll treat it better on the night of the ball."

He produced a small but full purse and plunked it onto my worktable. That did a little bit to ease the sting of having the dress returned for repairs within a day.

"Sure she will," I muttered. "Thank you for bringing it back here, my boy. My old back appreciates it."

He laughed.

"Do you need my help with the repairs?"

"No, no. I'll work on this tomorrow. It is far too late to do any work on this tonight, and I have other plans for the evening."

I glanced at the large man who leaned on the wall just inside my workshop, struggling to resist biting my lip where Finn could see it. The boy was a notorious gossip and Cormac's employee besides. Finn looked confused. He glanced between Cormac and I several times before realization, and a grin, dawned on his sweet face.

"I will leave you two alone, then. Don't have too much fun. We all have work tomorrow."

I rolled my eyes. Stuffing his hands in his pockets, he began to whistle a jaunty tune I was fairly certain he'd heard from a busker and made his way out of the shop. Turning back to Cormac, I realized that he'd stepped further into the room while I was watching Finn leave. He was standing next to my work chair, resting his hand comfortably on the back. I let my eyes rove over his powerful muscles, relishing the sight of him. He truly was one of the most handsome men I'd ever seen.

"You know he's going to tell every single one of your shop girls about us, right? I think any hope of secrecy you might have had about us just walked out the door with him."

I shrugged, putting a little bit of sway into my step as I walked towards him. It seemed to work. Even in the dim light of the room, I could see Cormac's eyes widen and darken with desire. When I replied, my voice was breathy in a way that I hadn't expected.

"I guess it's a good thing that I didn't have any intention of keeping us a secret."

He reached out his hand to me and I placed my hand in his open palm. Clasping my palm, he pulled me gently toward him.

"Poppy, I don't want to hide this from the world either. I want... so much."

His other hand gently caressed my cheek. I couldn't help taking a deep breath of the scent of metal and sweat that clung to his skin and wrapped my arms around his bulky waist. I had always loved how much larger he was than me, especially when we were close like this. I wanted so much with him, too.

Now that there were romantic feelings openly involved, the contact was even more meaningful. My pulse raced as I looked up at him through my eyelashes. When he pulled away, he looked down at me as if I were the most precious metal he'd ever beheld. I never wanted this to end.

"Cormac... what do you say we skip the drink tonight? Take me to bed."

He kissed me and I groaned, my need for him making itself known in the pit of my stomach.

"Your wish is my command," he growled. It was the sexiest sound I'd ever heard. Without waiting, he lifted me so my legs were at his waist, and began his way upstairs.

7

I was supposed to be responding to letters. Instead, I had been musing on some poetry that I wanted to write for Genevieve.

A knock sounded on my open door and I glanced up to see one of the palace servants stick their head through the door of my study. I slid the page of half written poetry under the stack of unused vellum.

"Apologies for the interruption, Your Grace, but I have the day's post for you. One of these letters is marked as urgent and I wanted to ensure it made it to your hands."

"Oh, perfect, I'd just finished this letter to be sent out. I'll trade you."

He handed me the thick stack of creamy vellum envelopes. I flipped over the envelope on top that was marked urgent, only to realize it was from Wolvington's seneschal, Bertrand. That was concerning.

There had been reports of unusually vicious wolves in the forests before I left and I had asked him to keep me posted. He was not one to exaggerate problems. I slipped my finger under the wax seal and pulled out the letter. True to form, the letter was terse; there were three lines in Bertrand's crisp hand followed by his initials.

Your Grace,

The problem with the wolves continues to worsen. Several of our soldiers have been injured to the point that we need your assistance. Please return home to assist us or send help.

BT

I grimaced. If they needed my help, it meant things were serious back at home. I would need to leave immediately if I was going to be able to help the soldiers who had been injured in time. I had to pack.

Trying to climb out of my chair without moving it, I tripped and barely caught myself before my face smashed into the floor. After last week's unfortunate concussion incident, I didn't want to spend any more time at the healers. Especially with my people depending on me.

Luckily, I didn't need much in the way of travel supplies. I knew routes that I could use to shave nearly a full day off of the journey that I had taken with my parents in the carriage. By traveling light, with only what I needed from the Palace healers to treat my people and enough food to get me there, it wouldn't be a difficult journey at all.

I just had to tell my mother where I was going. That would be the difficult part, as she would have to make my excuses for all of the social engagements that Bayard had scheduled me for. At least I had a good reason for it this time. Not even my much older brother could find fault with me going back home to take care of a serious problem like this. Or so I hoped.

***

AVERY

I rode hard through the night and had gotten started early again in the morning after a few hours' rest. If there was anything I was glad for, it was the fact that it didn't take as long to reach home on horseback as it did by carriage. The countryside was beginning to blossom into spring as I rode through it. Leaves were beginning to regrow on the oaks of the forest.

I had no idea what kind of situation I would be getting into once I got home. If Bertrand had called for my help, there would be at least a few people injured fairly severely. Otherwise our staff healers would be well able to handle animal bites, even from a wolf.

My horse's galloping kicked up the dark brown dirt that our region was famous for. Wolvington was known for its thick forests and prize rams and sheep. We had some of the best breeding stock in Elisade, and supplied a good chunk of the country's wool. As a result, we tended to have more than enough money to live off of as a duchy. But the sheep were also a draw for the packs of wolves that roamed our forests, especially in lean winters that were especially cold.

The fact that these wolves were being so vicious, and so consistent, worried me. Usually, the furry beasts did their best to stay far away from the areas that we patrolled. As long as they left us alone, we left them alone. This was the third bunch of attacks we'd had on soldiers, but the first time anyone had been seriously injured. Something wasn't right about this but I couldn't put my finger on it.

I had to slow my horse down as we got further into the forest. I didn't want to risk the gelding picking up a stone or tripping over a tree root while we were so far from anyone who could help to heal him. I knew the basics of wrapping a tender hoof, but if he broke or sprained something out here, it would add nearly half a day to my journey, instead of taking few hours at best which I couldn't afford at the moment. My people needed me, and that was the most important thing on my mind.

It didn't stop me from wishing I had written a small missive to Genevieve to tell her that I would be out of town for a few days. I just hadn't thought to do it before I left and now it was too late. I hoped she would forgive me for the lapse in manners.

Thoughts of her filled my mind as I guided my horse through the familiar woods. I wondered what she would think of Wolvington. Teagan wasn't all that different, being essentially neighbors, though they tended to focus more on agrarian products than we did. As I thought of all the places at home that I wanted to show her, the woods around me began to thin.

Glimpses of sandstone walls and wooden buildings began to show through the trees and my heart beat a little bit faster. I was home. There was no more time to waste. Kicking the gelding into a trot, I began to steel myself for the situation ahead of me.

Guards moved to stop me as I came up to the gate, until they recognized me. Then they saluted. I didn't recognize either of them, but that wasn't a surprise. We regularly rotated guards throughout different areas of the duchy in order to ensure that there were no issues of bribes or other corruption among their ranks.

"Welcome home, Your Grace."

I nodded to the two soldiers. Sliding off the horse, I handed the reins to one of them and began to pull things out of my saddlebags.

"Bertrand sent for me after the latest attack," I explained. "Where are the wolf survivors located?"

"The garrison hospital, Your Grace. Do you require help carrying your things?"

"Yes, please. I brought medical supplies from the palace, so my bags are as full as I could get them. And stop that 'Your Grace' nonsense. We haven't time for it."

"Would you like to visit your rooms first or head straight to the hospital? Bertrand informed us you were coming to help with the attacks."

"The hospital, please."

Nodding, one of the soldiers detached the bags from the saddle entirely. I blinked. That would've been the smart way to handle this situation. With a short bow, he spoke.

"Follow me, sir."

The gates opened and he led me through the maze that was the garrison's section of the duchy. Wooden buildings of varying sizes lined the gravel walkways that were made of smaller pieces of the same stone that built the walls. I hadn't spent much time in this part of the duchy, as security had been one of my father's duties since he came to Wolvington before I was born.

However, I knew a hospital when I saw one. The long, segmented building with a handful of windows on both sides had been rebuilt from the ground up several years ago per the latest in medical technology. It had a ward for contagious diseases and one for the general injuries like the occasional broken bone, animal bites or concussions that were common in soldiers on duty, with curtains between the beds for privacy.

I walked in to find that the curtains were drawn around every single one of the forty beds that made up the two wards. Bertrand certainly had not been exaggerating. I could hear soft voices behind them, but I didn't see anyone. Where was the healer that had been assigned to this garrison? Where were the nurses who should have been assisting them? I turned to the soldier who had guided me to ask, only to find that he was staring at one of the beds in horror. Following his gaze, I recoiled.

The body wrapped in the blankets barely resembled a human being at all. What had once been bare flesh was now covered in thick gray and brown fur, all the way to the person's hands which were now clenched into what could have been fists, except that they were tipped with black claws. My healing instincts kicked in as I looked at him. Two healers stood on opposite sides of the bed, holding him down.

A glint of silver peeked out from the fur covering his torso. In a flash, I ripped the silver pendant away from his flesh. I didn't know exactly why I had done it, but everyone standing beside me stared along with me as the fur and claws began to recede into his body. The animals that had attacked them had not been your average wolves. They had been werewolves. This was going to be a much bigger problem than I had anticipated.

GENEVIEVE

It had been almost a week since the date with Avery, but I had yet to hear from him. I had sent a messenger to the Palace inviting him to a dinner with our family, but we had received no word from him. It was nerve-wracking.

To take my mind off of all things romantic, Alys had finally followed through on her threat to take me shopping for new, more fashionable outfits for the rest of the season and for general wear. She was nearly bouncing on her toes as we walked through the merchants' district. I had to admit, her joy was infectious. I couldn't keep the small smile off of my face.

I was glad that Mama had not been able to join us, which was certainly something I wouldn't have found myself thinking just a few weeks ago. It had been a long time since the two of us had spent any real time together, between her studies, my knighthood, and our inability to be alone for longer than five minutes without arguing. This morning, however, had been peaceful so far. We had breakfasted at home and had the carriage drop us off near the entrance of the district.

I couldn't help but feel a pang remembering the last time I had been here with Avery. Alys seemed to sense it and had told me she would keep me so busy I wouldn't even have time to miss him. So far, her promise had been accurate. We had already been in a handful of stores as we made our way to the center of the district where I suspected we would find what she was looking for. She had always loved clothes that were as beautiful as they were expensive.

Not that either of us had a real goal in mind for the outfits we sought. I found myself wanting to buy more of the skirts in the Fraisian style that Alys had shown me, but we hadn't found a tailor that was skilled in creating them yet.

"I have a good feeling about this next shop," Alys told me as we left yet another mediocre shop. "Andreas has always been on the forefront of fashion here in the city. I'm sure ze will have something beautiful for us to try on."

"Here's to hoping," I sighed. "By the way, how did the meeting with Ianto go last week?"

"Oh, it went well. He scolded me for spending so much of my own funds on my experiments, but you know how it is. Quality ingredients make for quality results, and when I'm in charge of other people's lives, I need quality results."

I laughed. I knew that well. Ianto had scolded me time and time again for spending "too much" on balms, armor and weapons during my squiredom. I had only been able to put a stop to his issues with my spending by taking him shopping with me a few times. Once he'd seen the price of quality weapons and armor, he'd shut up.

"Honestly, I can't wait to see his face when he sees the price of the gown I commissioned," I laughed. "And then the repairs? Oh, he'll be hopping mad. But Mama approved the costs, so he can bite me."

"Not to mention you're taking part in the time-honored tradition of a possible arranged marriage," Alys reminded me then clapped a hand over her mouth. "Goddess, I am so sorry. I forgot we weren't talking about Avery today."

I waved her concern off, until a deep, feminine voice rang out of the open windows of a shop just ahead of us. When I saw who was calling out to us, I nearly fainted.

"Is that Alys of Teagan I hear?" Duchess Celeste of Wolvington poked her head out of the shops window and beamed at us. "It is! Oh, and this must be Ser Genevieve. I have been wanting to meet you! Please, both of you come in and tell me what you think of these dresses Andreas has created for me!"

It was clear from her tone, and her position as the King Father's wife, that it was not a request. As soon as she ducked back into the shop, I whirled on my younger sister, fury building in my chest.

"Did you know she would be here?" I hissed, trying desperately to keep my words quiet so that the Duchess wouldn't hear. "Was this supposed to be a fun surprise? 'Cause I've gotta tell you, it's not fun."

Alys's eyes and mouth were wide open in what looked like surprise. This is the exact sort of thing I'd been dreading when I'd asked for her help.

"I had no idea! I mean, Avery told me that his mother was a frequent client of Andreas's but I didn't know she would be here today! Gen, you have to believe me!"

Pinching the bridge of my nose, I realized something. I believed her.

This was something that she might have done when we were a decade younger, but she had really grown out of her pranks in the last few years. Knowing how anxious I was about everything involving Avery, I couldn't imagine the Alys that stood before me planning something like this without telling me. Dropping my hand, I took a few deep breaths.

"Okay. I believe you."

"You do?" Alys was still staring at me in surprise.

"I do. But you have to help me out in there. I've never actually talked to her before. Only guarded her as a squire."

"Of course! We're a team."

My younger sister beamed at me, and I couldn't help but smile back at her. With her by my side, I thought I might just survive this encounter.

GENEVIEVE

Andreas's shop was overwhelming from the instant Alys and I stepped in. It was packed full of people of all sorts in all stages of purchasing tailored clothes, not to mention overflowing shelves. By the time we reached where Duchess Celeste stood by the open window, we were grateful for the fresh air. I was astonished she had been able to hear the conversation we'd been having from the noise in the room.

"My lady, I'm surprised to find you here today!" Alys swept to the older, stately woman and pressed a kiss to each of her rosy cheeks. "I thought for sure you'd have more important tasks to tend to on one of your rare visits to the capital."

"Yes, well, I thought to buy some new things while I was here, but apparently the entire city had the same idea. But it is no matter! I'm glad to see you, dear. And this must be your sister?"

Her eyes found mine and I dropped into the appropriate curtsy. I honestly couldn't believe I was standing there next to the woman who had produced Avery. She was as beautiful as I had expected her to be, with her dark braids hanging loose around her shoulders, wooden beads on the end.

"It's a pleasure to meet you, Your Grace. I've heard a lot about you."

"Oh, I'm sure you have. Alys here is full of tales of me messing up her experiments and causing general mayhem."

Her brown eyes were warm and glittering as she looked me up and down. She smiled at me and winked. I could see the resemblance between her and the man I'd been enjoying flirting with.

"I only told her the really good stories, I promise," Alys chirped. "I didn't want to scare her off from marrying into your family before she had the chance to meet you for real."

"Ah yes. I suppose that would be reasonable. But now you've met me. I'm not nearly as terrifying as the gossips would make me out to be, don't you think?"

She looked at me expectantly and I blushed, lowering my gaze.

"No, Your Grace. You seem perfectly lovely."

She clicked her tongue and I looked up to see her still smiling at me. I couldn't resist smiling back, even when one of the shop's workers joined us where we stood.

"Hello, Your Grace and ladies. It's my pleasure to serve you today. Do we have any particular clothes we're looking for?"

Alys and I deferred to the Duchess, who was all too happy to tell him what she wanted.

"I am searching for the perfect gown for the Prince's ball. Andreas said ze was going to make up a couple of options for me."

He nodded.

"Of course, Your Grace. Please follow me. We have a dressing room prepared for you, and we can help your companions find something that suits their needs as well."

Duchess Celeste nodded to him and he led us all through the maze of the store. I found myself liking the woman more and more as we talked. Maybe this wouldn't be so bad after all.

GENEVIEVE

By the time we arrived home, I was exhausted. I was fairly certain that we had tried on every gown ever created, and when you added on the general anxiety I had felt over spending the afternoon with someone I hoped would be my mother-in-law? Today had been a lot. Even Alys was less excitable than usual.

I intended to spend the remainder of the afternoon soaking myself until my skin wrinkled, eating dinner alone and then beat the snot out of the guards in our regular evening sparring matches.

Judging by the gleeful expression on my mother's face, that was not going to happen. Alys and I exchanged glances and groaned in sync.

"You two are home just in time! Your cousins from Bryn Eirian are here for the ball and will be staying with us. It's nearly time for a family dinner."

For the second time today, my jaw dropped in surprise. I had always hated surprises. When I spoke, my voice was flat.

"Did you know they were coming?"

Mama shrugged.

"We invited them but didn't know when they would arrive. One of their servants rode ahead this morning to give us warning, but you two were already gone for the day."

I pinched the bridge of my nose, trying to hide my annoyance. I didn't do a very good job of it. Alys spoke up.

"Mama, perhaps they would prefer not to dine so formally tonight? I know Genevieve would. We ran into Duchess Celeste while we were out today and Genevieve's pretty exhausted."

"Oh, no, both Ambrose and Oriol have been resting and are ready to have the best food we can provide here in the city," Mother replied.

I held back a groan. That was sure to mean a full, multi-course dinner. I liked my cousin and his new spouse well enough but I was *tired*.

Feeling Alys's gaze on me, I dropped my hand from in front of my face. I wasn't sure what she was looking for as she studied my face, but she apparently found it before turning back to our mother, her back straight.

"We'll need to delay dinner for at least an hour if you want us at dinner. Genevieve and I both need baths and time to decompress. If not, you can make our excuses to our cousins."

I blinked, surprised by her declaration. This was the first time she'd ever made such a case for both of us, not just herself. Mama turned to me, her eyes narrowed.

"Genevieve, is that what you want?"

"It is. I am desperately in need of some time for myself before I speak to another human being."

"Well. I will go tell the servants to delay the meal then."

I nearly fell to the floor in relief and gratefulness to my sister as my mother walked away. Despite my best efforts, I had never been able to stand up to my mother the way she had just done. Goblins, trolls, Linbournese troops? Piece of cake. Disagreeing with my mother over something as simple as the dinner schedule? Not a chance.

Alys still stood next to me, her entire body at ease like what she had just done was no big deal. I was amazed.

"Thank you so much. I could *not* have handled dinner with the whole family right now."

She wrapped my hand in both of hers and squeezed gently, unexpectedly bringing tears to my eyes.

"There's no need to thank me. You and I are a team. I'm supposed to help take care of you, remember? Now go get into the bath before she changes her mind."

Laughing, I wiped my eyes with my hands and rushed to the back of the house where the bathing chambers were. It was nice to have Alys as an ally.

AVERY

My head was swimming, my back ached and I was *exhausted.* After discovering that my soldiers weren't being attacked by your regular forest variety of wolves and sending word to my cousin to send help, I had spent that evening, and the whole next day in the library reading everything there was to be found about every sort of unusual wolf. At that point, Bertrand nearly dragged me from the library and into my bed with a promise to wake me in six hours.

I had never dealt with anything like this before, even during my apprenticeship to the palace healers after graduation. I had always thought werewolves were a myth, but clearly I was mistaken. Now that I was awake and thinking more clearly, I knew it had been the right thing to do. I couldn't help anybody if I was asleep on my feet. Not to mention, the longer I went without sleep, the worse my handwriting got. If I had gone on any longer without a nap, not even I would've been able to read the notes I'd taken.

Now that I was properly awake, I could turn these notes into something that resembled a healing plan. Hopefully. There were a lot more of them than I remembered writing. I started to lay the pages out on the table in front of me, then realized that wouldn't work to help me visualize it the way I needed to. The realization of what I needed came to me in a flash. I snapped my fingers and a servant popped out from behind the shelves. I couldn't help but wonder how long she'd been there, but decided to save that question for later.

I needed my large cork board and three different colors of yarn. It was the best way for me to see everything and make connections between everything on the different pages. It had gotten me through my years at the Academy and much of my best spell work. I was sure it would work for this, too. After explaining what I needed, she scurried off to get them. I got back to organizing my notes.

After a few minutes, I heard the creak of the wheels that made my cork board mobile and several more sets of footsteps than I was expecting. Turning, I was surprised to see the servant bearing a basket of yarn and two people in healer's robes shuffling behind her with the cork board in tow. I didn't recognize either of them, but judging by the dark circles under their eyes and furrowed brows, they'd gotten even less sleep than I had. I frowned.

"What's the matter? Has something happened to the soldiers?"

They exchanged confused glances, but didn't say anything. The servant cleared her throat.

"Your Grace, these two healers came straight from the palace to assist you."

Both of them nodded. The taller of the two reached their hand out and spoke in a gruff voice, introducing them both. They must have ridden from the palace within an hour of getting my message in order to be standing here right now.

"I'm Tomas and this is Vincent. You should refer to both of us with masculine pronouns. Knight Commander Cedric sent us at your letter."

He had a strong grip. I was surprised to hear him roll his words together in a Fraisian accent but let it go. The amulets around their necks bore the distinct magical aura marking them as palace healers.

"A pleasure to meet you both. I'm Duke Avery of Wolvington, but I don't stand on formality with other healers. Call me Avery and use masculine pronouns, please." When they both nodded, I continued. "Have either of you ever treated werewolf victims before? I did all the research I could to see what there was to be found-"

Vincent cut me off. His features and general expression reminded me of a lightning bolt - delicate but determined - but his voice was light and reedy.

"Show us your research and we will share what we know. It has been a long time since anyone has treated werewolf attacks in this country and the only notes we were able to find were... incomplete."

That was odd. I knew it had been a while since there had been an attack, but usually the palace scholars kept all healing notes well organized.

"Give me half an hour to get myself set up and I'll be able to show you. You two must have ridden hard. Would you to like to sleep for a while before we begin working?"

They exchanged glances again then shook their heads at the same time.

"We are both accustomed to little sleep while working. If there are couches in here, we will rest there until you are ready for us."

Without requiring a command, the servant who had brought them to me made her way out of the room.

"Of course. Can we offer you any food or drink? Anything you need within reason while you are here is at your disposal."

Tomas smiled a thin, toothless smile.

"I believe that your cook has already taken pity on us and will send someone up with a tray momentarily."

Apparently my confusion showed on my face. His eyes tracked the movement of the servants who were rearranging the furniture to allow for the couches to be out of direct sunlight but near enough that I could reach them without hunting for them.

"We came up through the servant's quarters," he explained. That made sense if they'd come from the main road instead of the forest route I'd taken. Coming up that way was the fastest way to get to the library. "Now, if you will excuse me, I would like to get some rest. It has been a hard journey and I suspect this healing work will be intense."

I nodded and he flopped unceremoniously onto the couch. Within moments, he had wrapped himself in the thick blanket the servants had provided and turned into the pillows on the back. Vincent was already snoring on his own couch across the room. It was time for me to get my research set up so that we could all understand what I had found and what they had brought with them.

I set to work, pinning all twelve pages of my work to the board quickly. That was the easy part. Now I had to read through them and see what actually made sense together, connecting things with yarn pinned to board. From there, I'd rewrite my notes into a page or two. Alys had compared this process to spinning a spiderweb, and she wasn't wrong. When I had worked at the Academy, I had had a room specifically for this. The walls were covered in cork so that I could do this on a larger scale. One project had been so intensive and required so much in the way of notes and yarn that I'd accidentally trapped myself in the room without realizing it. I smiled at the memory as I worked, chewing lightly on one of the pins I would use later. It helped me focus, though my mother had told me that it was not one of my more attractive traits.

Reading back over my notes, nearly every book had mentioned an issue with silver, though none of them had actually agreed on why or how it affected anything with the transformation. I realized that the silver necklace I had pulled off of the man in the hospital was still in my pocket. I hadn't taken much time to look at it before, but it couldn't hurt to add it to the board along with everything else. I pulled the thin chain from my pocket and rubbed the pendant between my thumb and forefinger. It was a simple but well-crafted circular drop with the goddess's sigil carved out of the center like those that many who were particularly religious wore - nothing particularly unusual for a soldier to wear.

I nearly dropped it when Vincent's voice came from behind me suddenly.

"You have done some good work here. May I see that?"

The much taller, light skinned man stepped forward, his hands in the pockets of his robes. I held it out to him without looking away from the board in front of us and he took it from me with gentle hands.

"From what we know of werewolf attacks, there isn't much we can do to stop them from turning into the creatures, but we can help them to avoid triggers - like this one."

He swung the pendant a few times for emphasis, then hung it from a pin on the board. It made sense. Chewing on the pin, I waited for him to continue, but he didn't.

"What are other known triggers for the transformations?"

"Funnily enough, wolfsbane. Much like silver, it acts as a poison when ingested, which causes the body to transform into its stronger form. There have been a few reports of rye causing the transformation as well. Other than that, they usually transform on the full moon."

I shook my head at the irony of it. It was good to know, though. I hoped that these people would be able to live fairly regular lives despite the result of the attacks. Knowing the triggers would help them to heal quickly, though the healers had mentioned that their physical wounds were healing much faster than any of them had expected. They suspected, and I agreed, it was likely because of the source of the attacks.

There was still the problem of how to deal with the ones that were still roaming the forests of Wolvington spreading this condition. I suspected that I would have to accept Cedric's help again with hunting the wolves down, though the thought of killing semi-human creatures who were likely once my responsibility left me ill at ease. Three attacks from the same group of them was enough for me to know it was needed.

The other problem was one that didn't have as easy a solution in my mind. I posed the question to my companion, while Tomas snored lightly on the couch.

"How do we keep them from attacking people the way they were?"

Vincent didn't answer me for several moments. He stood, staring at the board in quiet contemplation. When he finally did speak, his voice was quiet.

"That is the question I've been trying to figure out myself. Usually, werewolves act like regular wolves when they transform. They avoid humans whenever possible unless they are incredibly low on food. As long as there is someplace nearby that's got plenty of game for them to hunt on the night of the full moon, there shouldn't be an issue."

"That is definitely something we can handle," I mused. It wouldn't be difficult to have people come in on the night of the full moon and have soldiers guard them to make sure nothing went awry. Especially since most of the new wolves were soldiers themselves.

A groan from the back of the room announced that Tomas had woken up. We looked back to see him rubbing his eyes with both hands before getting up. He kept the blanket around his shoulders.

"Why didn't you wake me? I didn't need the sleep...whoa." The short, stocky man stopped short when he saw the work I had done. "That is one of the more interesting methods I've seen someone use for their notes."

"That's one of the least rude ways I've heard someone discuss it." I grinned at him and the ghost of a smile played on his lips. "We didn't talk about the healing plan yet, so you didn't miss much. Would you like to start us off?"

With a nod, he picked up the stack of papers he had brought in with him and flipped through them. Apparently finding what he was looking for, he took a deep breath and began speaking to us both. I gave him my full attention.

"Werewolves heal quickly, as your healers have no doubt noticed. However, that can often mean that their wounds do not heal well. If a bone is broken or something gets lodged in their flesh, the bone can often set badly or heal around the problems. With that in mind, here's what I propose..."

8

AVERY

The sun was rising over the ocean as I passed through the city gates, and I was still entirely exhausted. I had been riding for way too long, stopping only twice to water the horse and stretch some feeling into my legs again. I needed to stop again, but I had no intention of doing so before I reached the palace. Nothing but a royal decree was going to keep me from the featherbed that was waiting for me for the few hours I had before I needed to start getting ready for Julian's ball. Hopefully, Bayard would be too busy to find anything else for me to do.

I wasn't the only one coming in at the last minute for the ball, judging by the dozens of carriages I had passed on the main road. However, they likely didn't smell of a combination of dust, human and horse sweat, thanks to their smarter traveling accommodations. I desperately wished there were a more efficient mode of travel that I could have used, but for now, this was the best we had.

There was no chance in hell I was going to miss out on a chance to see Genevieve in that dress again, preferably when she wasn't pointing a pair of sharp blades at me.

CORMAC

On the day of the Prince's ball, one of Poppy's shop girls came running into the forge. The bell over the door jangled so hard that I thought it might fall off.

"Isabella, what is the matter?" Finn asked. Concern was clear in his voice, and I could see why. Isabella's simple, yet cleverly decorated dress was covered in dust and she was very out of breath. "Is Poppy all right?"

The girl raised a thumb to us in affirmation, then bent over, trying to catch her breath. Finn set aside the decorative iron work that he was working on and rushed to her side, offering his arm for her.

"Poppy is fine...but we need your help to deliver that blasted knight's gown to the palace. Maria and I aren't strong enough, and Poppy doesn't trust us with the other gown they have to deliver."

A laugh ripped its way out of my chest. Poppy would send their shop girl running like her life depended on it over a gown delivery. I can see from the way her back was straight, even as she struggled to breathe, that she was wearing a corset. It could not have been a comfortable run from the shop to the forge.

"That's something we can easily do," I told her. "Finn, get Isabella some water and help her get her dress cleaned up. You two can meet us at the palace. I'll head over to the shop and help Poppy. I am sure they will need Isabella's help to perfect the gown for Lady Alys once we arrive."

Finn nodded firmly and took the lead with Isabella. I ran my fingers through my hair, slipped my coat on and started on my way to my partner's shop. It felt good to think those words. My partner. Even if we hadn't said them out loud yet. I was enjoying this new aspect to our relationship, even when it meant something as normal as helping them with the delivery.

As soon as Poppy had realized they needed to do repairs on Ser Genevieve's gown, they had wondered about the logistics of delivering it and the gown for Lady Alys. I couldn't wait to see the finished product for both gowns. Poppy did wonderful work and I was bursting with pride at the thought that the Teagan heirs would be showing it off tonight.

I was also proud in a weird way of how both of the heirs to the duchy he'd grown up in had turned out. It'd been a long time since they had watched me from the forge's front room, asking me all kinds of questions.

They were famous for their fights even then, which I supposed was the way of things when one sister grew up a sorcerer and the other a knight. Lady Alys kept everything closer to the vest than her sister did, for all she was constantly running around having all sorts of fun.

The lady was constantly being gossiped about wherever she was, but I hadn't heard anything of Ser Genevieve that I recalled until she'd walked into my shop, glorious as the morning sun. Both gowns would suit them and their differences.

As Poppy's shop came into view, I could see them pacing back and forth between their shop's arched double doors and window. I began to whistle one of my favorite tunes and Poppy halted in the open window. I couldn't see it, but I knew exactly what the scowl on their face would look like and I loved it.

"Come on now, old man!" They called irritably. "We don't have all afternoon to get these gowns to the Teagan's! Put some pep in your step!"

I laughed, lengthening my strides and closing the distance

between myself and the whitewashed building quickly. Poppy would be tapping their foot in irritation while they waited for me. As I got closer, I could see the way that the bright afternoon sun glanced off of their skin, deepening their frown lines and showing off just how bright their eyes were.

Just looking at them brought a silly grin to my face. I tried to cover it by running my hands around the edges of my beard, but there was no mistaking the love that pounded through my veins.

"You're completely done in, aren't you, mate?" I muttered to myself with a shake of my head. "You've gone and fallen head over heels for your friend. How silly is that?"

I was far too old to be mooning about like an apprentice. We had a job to do and there was no time for foolishness.

When I reached the door, Poppy was in fact tapping their foot impatiently. Behind them stood two mannequins with the gowns we were set to transport.

"Did Isabella not tell you that this was an emergency? I look out and see you moseying along the road like we've got nowhere to be!"

I held my hands out to them in apology. I was glad that they weren't covered in soot and sweat for once. It wouldn't have been the first time that Poppy made me wash myself from head to toe before coming in, and it certainly wouldn't have been the last. Forge smoke and soot had a magical power to get on everything you didn't want it to.

"Isabella did tell me it was an emergency, but I didn't want be unable to breathe once I got here, like she was when she got to my forge. You know you scared that poor girl half to death."

Poppy sniffed and rolled their eyes.

"A little bit of fear is good for the soul. Besides, it'll give Finn a reason to be the mighty protector as he likes to be. Consider it my contribution to their romance."

I shook my head at them.

"You, my dear, are ridiculous."

"And a skilled matchmaker, as you well know. The only people who leave my shop unmarried are those who have no interest in it or have not met anyone they are interested in having a marriage with. Isabella falls under neither of those categories."

"And what about yourself?"

The words slipped out before I could stop them. I clapped a hand over my mouth but there was no taking them back. Luckily, they laughed.

"I defy all rules, my good man, but I have not left this shop behind just yet. There's plenty of time."

I looked up as they spoke, and Poppy winked at me. My heart skipped a beat.

"Now, we really are in a hurry. Help me and Maria load these gowns into bags, would you?"

In my haste to feel less awkward and do what I was told, I nearly tripped over my feet on my way to the mannequins. Biting back curses that I knew Poppy wouldn't appreciate, I quickly unlaced the shiny black gown and shimmied it over the mannequin's shoulders.

Maria held the garment bag open and Poppy pressed the fluttering gown into it so that it wouldn't be damaged or wrinkled when we got there. We repeated the process with the chainmail gown, though this time I held the bag. For something that was half silk, this gown was heavy. I was fairly certain that I've made full suits of armor that were lighter than this gown was now that it was finished. However, there was no chance they were anywhere near as pretty. Poppy had done wonderful work.

"All right," Poppy clapped. "Maria, you carry Lady Alys's gown, and Cormac, can you carry Ser Genevieve's? I'll get my kit ready and we can have this delivered and perfected."

"After you, boss," Maria said unenthusiastically. Poppy beamed at us both and grabbed their woven reed basket from beside the door, leading the way through it with a bounce in their step.

GENEVIEVE

Alys and I were going to wear paths in the carpet attached to our rooms at the palace. Alys had never been good at waiting and the stress that was radiating off of my younger sister was adding into my own.

"When will they arrive?" Alys fretted, worrying the edges of her sleeves between her manicured fingers. The pointed tips had been painted the mulberry of their house crest for the evening, standing out against the light, lilac dressing gown she wore.

"It's early yet," I reminded her gently. "I'm sure they're already on their way."

"But what if the gown is terrible?"

"Didn't you go and look at it just a few days ago? You told Mother you loved it."

"Well, yes, but-"

I cut her off.

"No buts. Even if the gown fits like a potato sack, and it won't, you have several others that you can make work, and you know it. Will you at least pretend to be calm?"

Alys growled wordlessly under her breath, but slowed her pace measurably, just in time for several short raps on the door. I called for them to come in, and was surprised to see my mother and Juniper standing in the doorway.

Duchess Vivienne stepped into the room and raised a single blonde eyebrow at her daughter's antics.

"I see we are taking the wait well. I suspected as much, and came prepared."

She gestured for Juniper to come forward, and Genevieve saw that they were carrying a large leather case in both hands.

"I am going to help you prepare for the ball," Vivienne declared. Juniper set the carrying case on the vanity with a loud thunk. I wasn't sure what was in it. The case had piqued Alys's curiosity as well, judging by how far she was craning her neck to see it.

"Instead of having the maids do your hair and makeup, I thought we'd have a little fun and I would do it for you!" Mama grinned, showing off sharp canines behind bright red lips.

A twinge of jealousy pinched at me as I looked at them. They were both so beautiful in a way I could never be, thanks to having my father's square build and a collection of scars from years spent practicing in the heat of the sun. It was something I had long since come to terms with, but tonight I was struggling with the comparisons.

Mama laid out her tools - a selection of small pots and brushes, as well as several metal implements that looked as if they would fit better in the king's dungeon than the dressing room we stood in.

"Now, who wants to go first?"

I thought for a moment, figuring out the logistics.

"Alys, why don't you go first, so that you're ready for the final fitting when the gowns arrive?"

Alys nodded, rising wordlessly from the chair she'd plonked down in.

"Anything is better than sitting here waiting with nothing to do," she declared as she swanned across the room. I didn't bother hiding my eye roll.

Now that Alys was preoccupied, it would be possible for me to focus on the book I'd been reading before she arrived. I slid into the chair that sat in the corner of the room. It had the best vantage point, with a direct view of the door and if I turned my head, I could watch my mother work.

Alys was perfectly capable of applying her own makeup, but had never been skilled with styling her own hair. Fortunately, Vivienne had always been great at convincing her daughters' curls into the court's fashionable styles, no matter how intricate.

"Mother, I'd like to have my hair in proper ringlets tonight, if that's all right?"

"Of course, darling! Why do you think I brought the irons? We'll start with your eyelids, so that the irons have time to heat properly, and so we don't get any lipstick on that beautiful gown you ordered. Sound good?"

Alys smiled at her mother in the mirror and closed her eyes obediently. I shook my head lightly, and turned my eyes back to the novel in my hands while I waited.

* * *

POPPY

A liveried servant who introduced themself as Juniper showed the three of us to another room in the palace, this time near the knight's barracks.

I couldn't remember a time in my life when I'd been this nervous, even when we'd done the last fitting for the knight. Cormac placed a hand at the small of my back and the warmth was reassuring.

I took a deep breath and nodded to Juniper. They rapped hard on the door.

"Come in," an unfamiliar woman's voice called jovially. "You have perfect timing! Alys is just about ready for you, and I cannot wait to see what the two of you have come up with for her!"

We walked in and I nearly dropped my basket at the sight of the duchess. Bowing low, I motioned for Maria to do the same.

"Duchess Vivienne, Lady Alys, you look lovely," Cormac told

her with a cheeky grin. "Ser Genevieve, you look quite well, as always."

"As do you, old friend!"

Genevieve shook his free hand, and welcomed us all into the room.

"You can lay the gowns down here," she said, pointing towards the small couch in the center of the room. "I hope that my repair needs were not too difficult for you, Poppy?"

I shot her a half-hearted glare. She smiled.

"I should have been prepared for it, knowing you had to test it out for the Knight Commander, but it wasn't the worst repair I've had to make in a quick turn."

"I'm glad it wasn't too bad for you. I do hate to make a fuss. I'm sorry, what's your name, dear?"

The last question was directed towards the young woman standing behind me.

"Oh, I'm Maria. I'm... I work for Poppy."

"We're glad to have you, Maria! Come in and stand by the fire for a moment. There's an awfully cold breeze coming off the ocean today, and I know you had a bit of a walk. Oh, Juniper, could you bring in some mulled wine and water to help them warm up?"

Juniper curtsied in response, and swept out of the room to do as they were asked. Cormac crossed the room in three steps, laying the garment bag he carried across the couch with a sigh of relief.

"I hope that that dress is less heavy to wear than it is to carry one-handed," he remarked. He stretched his arms out across the room, nearly able to touch both Genevieve and Alys with each hand. The room was relatively large, but with all six of them in there, it was pretty crowded. I hoped we'd be able to get both women into the gowns without any issue.

As if knowing I was thinking about her, Alys rose from the vanity chair and turned to face the crowded room. I couldn't help but stare open mouthed.

"Alys, you look *wonderful*," Genevieve breathed.

"There's no need for such a tone of surprise," Alys replied acidly. Judging by the twinkle and the small smile on her painted lips, she didn't mean it.

"Genevieve, darling, come and sit. Juniper will be back with their wine any moment now, and they'll need Alys so that they can get her dress to be as perfect as yours is."

Maria stepped closer to the couch, clearing a path for Genevieve and Alys to change places. I picked up the garment bag that my assistant had carried in. As the bag dropped to the floor, it was Alys's turn to gasp at the sight before her.

"Oh, Poppy, tell me that's my gown!"

I beamed back at her, pride swelling in my chest. The gown was a vision in black, designed to cling to the lady's ample bosom and wide hips. If it worked as I'd intended - and it would - it would make her look as if she were floating in the layers of nearly translucent black fabric. The sleeves of the gown were mere slips of ribbon with more of the dress's material hanging from it. It wouldn't cover her shoulders at all, which would have been scandalous only a year or two before, but would be perfectly fashionable now.

"Oh, Alys, it's perfect for you!" Genevieve squealed. "Try it on, quickly! I want to see this before Mother gets me into her clutches."

The duchess laughed, barely holding back what looked like tears. Her hands were clasped together in front of her own chest, a gesture that was rare on the restrained matriarch of the family.

Juniper opened and closed the dressing room's door with one hand, balancing the tray of wine they'd been sent to fetch with the other. It was clearly something they were skilled with, I couldn't help but note. It was impressive.

"That's my cue to leave, I reckon," Cormac said hastily, grabbing a cup as he made his way out the door. "Poppy, I will meet you two in the kitchen whenever you are ready to leave, okay?"

I nodded, my heart full of love and affection for the man walking away from me. I wrenched my gaze away from his retreating form and back to the women in my charge.

"Come on, then, let's get you dressed."

GENEVIEVE

The heavy wooden door of the barracks closed with a thud behind me. There had been raucous conversation when I'd opened the door, but now that people could see me, it had quieted to a roaring silence.

I looked down, noticing that the scabbards for my short swords were causing the silk of my skirt to pucker. I adjusted them, smoothing the deep blue silk with shaking hands. When I looked up, nearly everyone in the room was staring at me, or at least it felt that way.

Some of the other Knights were staring unabashedly. Ser Raoul was grinning at me from his bunk. I have never heard the room this quiet. After a few moments that felt like years, one of the older female knights spoke up from a table in the center of the long room.

"Can you actually fight in that?"

"Yeah, she can!" Raoul whooped.

That prompted the room to break into conversation again, rising to its usual level of noise. I breathed a sigh of relief.

He was never one to turn down the chance to tell a good story. Raoul gave a dramatic recounting of the previous week's duel, complete with screams, googly eyes and flailing about. It had the entire room rolling with laughter, including me.

It broke the stunned atmosphere of the room, and everything went more or less back to normal. Three of my fellow knights swarmed up to me, wanting to look at the dress. I giggled and twirled, showing off my movement skills within the dress.

"I cannot believe old Iron Britches agreed to even let you try this," one of the older women called. I craned my neck to see who was speaking and saw Ser Allondra grinning at me.

Ser Allondra had been one of the first non-noble applicants to earn her title several decades before. She had also been one of my mentors early on, having opted to come back to the city and palace to work after she had done ten years of service with the Army. She joked that she had spent so much time teaching the new recruits that she might as well get paid extra to do it while serving the crown. I adored her.

"What do you think?"

I twirled for my mentor, trying to hide how nervous I was. She studied me.

"I think it's lovely," Allondra granted. "It's a little frilly for my tastes, but you know I've never been one for dresses in a general way. It suits you."

"You really think so?"

"I would not have said it if I didn't. Now come and help me strap into my plate mail. Unless you intend on swanning about and flirting with all of these fine fellows all night."

She smirked up at me and I felt myself blush.

"Oh, you do intend on flirting then, do you? Have you finally gotten up the courage to speak to the Duke?"

"We went to lunch, I'll have you know, and then had a lovely time shopping for birthday presents for Alys."

Allondra guffawed, punching me in the arm lovingly.

"And you didn't turn into a frog or anything! Good for you, Genevieve! I'll be sure to make sure you two have time for a dance or two this evening, then, same as I've done for the rest of these lugs while they were courting."

I grinned at her.

"Let's get you dressed, shall we? We can't leave Prince Julian waiting for his escort to the ball."

9

AVERY

The guests were milling around the ballroom chattering amongst themselves when trumpets blared from the far side of the room. The bright melody announced the entrance of the royal family.

I took a deep breath and beamed as my family entered the room. I was so proud of Julian. He looked like a younger version of Father, from the long chestnut hair swept back into a low ponytail to the beak-like nose beneath deep brown eyes.

Julian could have passed for Old Man Winter in the crisp white suit with an icy blue tie that made his light brown skin and dark brown hair stand out beautifully.

Behind him came King Bayard and Queen Ines, looking as regal as ever. They too had taken the winter theme to heart, though the Queen was never without a pop of color in her own wardrobe. She had chosen a plush deep forest green gown that offset her lily pale skin beautifully clinging to her lithe form until it reached her hips. The lights in the room glinted off of the gold beaded collar that also served as the gown's only sleeves.

Beside her, Bayard wore a pale blue double-breasted tailcoat over crisp white trousers. His jacket was a slightly deeper blue than his son's. His sword hung at his side from a belt that matched his wife's gown. My serious older brother had allowed simple golden epaulets, with beaded tassels hanging around his shoulders, to be added to his tailcoat, along with several of his military medals. He cut a striking figure, just the hint of a shadow of facial hair that outlined his strong, square jaw.

As soon as they had fully entered the room, the honor guard swept in behind them. A dozen knights formed a semicircle behind the royal family, the lights reflecting brightly off of their plate mail and dress uniforms. I craned my neck, trying to catch a glimpse of Genevieve. It didn't take much to find her. She was standing directly in the center of the protective semicircle next to my old friend Ser Allondra of Brulport.

While her focus was on the royal family, as it should've been, Allondra's gaze was fixed on me. She gave me a small smile that no one else would notice unless they were looking. She turned her head ever so slightly and her mouth moved.

I had no idea what she was saying, but it soon became clear that she was trying to get Genevieve's attention. Genevieve's eyes found mine and I couldn't keep the smile off of my face.

She was stunning in the gown she'd had crafted. I had thought her beautiful before, but there was something slightly dangerous about her when she wore the chainmail gown. Something I couldn't help but be attracted to, even if I'd wanted to avoid catching feelings.

Her hair had been braided into a coil that circled the back of her head like a crown, and someone had woven in small crystals and bronze leaves that tied in to the decor on her pauldrons and bodice. It made her look delicate, but fierce at the same time. If someone had asked me to make her look more beautiful with my glamour skills, there was absolutely nothing I would change.

A hand pressed down on my shoulder and I jumped. Whirling, I was greeted by a familiar face.

"She looks great, doesn't she?" Alys bragged. Her face was alight with pleasure. "And you look good too, man!"

"Thanks! Genevieve does look wonderful. Almost as wonderful as she did before she knocked me out in the dueling ring."

I laughed, tugging at the suddenly too tight collar of my burnt sienna shirt.

"Almost as?" Alys cocked a well-shaped eyebrow. "Man, you are well suited for my sister if her being violent is what gets you going."

Now I laughed earnestly.

"You're in rare form tonight, Alys - and looking fabulous yourself, I might add."

It was true. Alys was always beautiful, but her dress enhanced everything I knew she loved about herself, and her makeup accented her light blue eyes and high cheekbones. The plunging neckline was drawing scandalized glances from some of the older nobles around them, but with the translucent mesh fabric covering everything, they couldn't say anything about it without looking prudish.

I loved it. The skirt floated around her ankles like a cloud, and I couldn't wait to see her really move in the dress. It would be a sight to behold.

The band struck up a simple tune that added to the low hum of conversation. Holding out my hand to Alys, I bowed.

"The family is here. Want to take a walk around the room with me and see if we see anyone from school?"

Alys took my hand and tucked it into her elbow. We made our

way across the room, pointing out people we knew. When we reached the far wall, Alys pulled away from me.

"Now, I have a confession. I came over here with a purpose other than to compliment you."

She looked oddly nervous. I tilted my head at her, curious.

"Oh?"

She scuffed the toe of her dancing shoe against the tile of the ballroom floor before speaking again.

"I wanted to come talk to you and make sure that you were going to ask Genevieve to dance tonight."

My eyebrows shot up.

"What are you, my mother? Does Genevieve's virtue need protection from me?"

"No, I already spoke to her this evening. Gen and I don't always get along, but she doesn't play games. I just want to make sure you aren't going to try and play any with her."

"I won't!"

She fixed me with a piercing glare.

"I swear to the goddess, Avery, if you are planning to mess around with her, I will hex you so that you will constantly be followed by the world's most annoying sound to you. I don't even know what it is but I will find out and it will follow you. You will never have peace and quiet again."

I knew she meant it. I placed my hand on Alys's bare shoulders and looked deeply into her eyes.

"Alys, I promise you I'm not here to play any games with Genevieve, unless they're ones she wants to play. I think we have the beginnings of a real connection. I'm not going to mess that up by playing coy."

That seemed to mollify her. Probably because it was the most honest I'd been with anyone other than Mother about how I'd begun to feel about Genevieve. It had been a long time since I'd found myself full of quite so many romantic feelings for someone. I genuinely cared for Genevieve and could see myself spending the rest of my life with her happily.

"So you are going to ask Gen to dance?"

I smiled softly and earnestly.

"As soon as I get the chance."

"Good, because I see Ser Antoni, and I want you to introduce me. Genevieve promised she would, but she's a little tied up, what with being in charge of the Prince's safety."

The change of topic was very typical for Alys. I shook my head at her and let my hands drop from her shoulders.

"I can introduce you to him. I don't think you'll like him once you've met him, though."

"See, I know that, but I also know that he's an absolutely divine dancer. Let a girl dream a little!"

I glanced over at the older knight. His luxurious salt and pepper locks flowed around the shoulders of his dress uniform. I had to admit he was very handsome, but Goddess, he was annoying.

He had a habit of sticking his nose in where it wasn't wanted - even when it led him to interrupting experiments and spells alike.

"Come on then, you atrocious flirt."

She beamed at me and I had to laugh. Walking her over to the older man, I pasted a charming smile onto my face before calling his attention.

"Antoni! Good to see you, old friend!"

GENEVIEVE

"Take a break, Ser Genevieve. I've got eyes on the family."

Allondra spoke brusquely, but the harshness was belied by the smirk that played across her face and the twinkle in her eye.

I opened my mouth to respond but heard footsteps coming from behind me. Whirling to face the sound, I had my sword half drawn before I heard Allondra's crackling laugh and recognized the man coming towards me. Avery.

I couldn't tell if my heart was skipping beats at the sight of him or just racing from the adrenaline rush that came with being snuck up on. If I was being honest, it was a combination of both. I let my sword slide back into its scabbard while I looked him over.

He cut a handsome figure in a navy blue tailcoat and trousers with a small, silver wolf head embroidered on the lapel. Unlike most of the men in the room, he didn't wear a decorative sword. Instead of a sword belt, there was a thin silver chain attaching a small dark leather satchel to the underside of his coat.

I couldn't help but notice that his outfit matched my gown almost perfectly. Had he done it on purpose? There was no way to tell.

I looked down, hoping to hide the blush that seemed to be ever present on my cheeks when he was near me. Tucking a stray hair back into my braid, I spoke.

"I wasn't sure I'd see you tonight. I hadn't heard much from you since the duel."

"Genevieve, I'm so sorry. I got your messages when I got back. I had... an urgent matter to deal with back on my own estate and didn't think to write before I left. I assure you, it won't happen again."

Again? That was a good sign. I bit my lip and smiled. He bowed.

"My humblest apologies, truly. I promise I won't go away without warning you next time."

He smiled at me and I knew my cheeks were getting even more pink. I cursed it a little.

I had spent my entire life training myself to have control over every muscle in my body. Unfortunately, my face had different ideas about what it wanted to do. It had apparently decided that, when it came to Avery, it was going to do its best to embarrass me. But he was still smiling at me. He reached up a hand and brushed his fingers against the back of my cheek.

Almost as if on cue, the band ended the upbeat courante they'd been playing, and transitioned into a much slower, more romantic chaconne. Around us, the other nobles sought their spouses and partners to join them on the dance floor while the horn and clarinet wove a simple, lilting melody around the dancers.

Avery bowed to me, so low that I could see the geometric pattern he'd shaved into the hair on the back of his head. When he rose, he held out his hand to me, palm up. His brown eyes were serious, but happy. I thought I could see another emotion in them, but I didn't quite recognize it.

I met his gaze, noticing the dimples that popped up with his wide smile and thought that I would be happy to spend all day looking at his face.

"May I have this dance, lady knight?"

I smiled and placed my palm in his. It was gratifying to realize that the suave, charming Duke of Wolvington's palms were as sweaty as mine. His touch sent a small spark through me that had nothing to do with his magical abilities.

"I would be delighted, my lord Duke."

***

GENEVIEVE

Our hands clasped, Avery and I made our way to the end of the rows of dancers. I was loath to let go of his hand, but it was required to dance a chaconne properly.

Squeezing his hand comfortingly, I released him to join the

ranks of the other people who would not be leading during this particular dance. Avery joined the other line directly across from me with a bow.

I curtsied to him, as was proper, and he grinned.

I am fairly certain I'm in love with those dimples, I thought, then amended my statement. *I am fairly certain I am falling in love with him entirely.*

The music picked up and I began to follow the dance pattern I had learned as a page. The chaconne was a simple dance made up of three basic steps, though there were more fanciful ones if you were a more skilled dancer than I.

Both groups of dancers moved in synch to the beat of the music, nearly double the speed of my heartbeat. Avery smiled softy at me as we circled each other, and I felt its warmth even when I couldn't see it. The gown swished and clanked around me as I moved, catching the eyes of the other dancers.

We wove around our neighbors in rows and squares, not sparing a second's attention for anyone but each other. I could tell that he was adapting to my simpler dance pattern from the small twirls and flourishes that he added to his own part.

It was more difficult than I'd expected to keep my arms in the raised position they needed to be in for this particular dance, thanks to the pauldrons that covered my shoulders. I was just grateful he hadn't asked me to join him for a minuet or an allemande, both of which required a lot more leaping than I was comfortable with in my current attire. However, I was definitely enjoying the view whenever Avery turned and leaped. His steps were elegant and graceful, with beautifully toned calves showing under his tailored pants.

My arms were starting to get stiff, making it a relief when the dance called for me and Avery to link arms. I loved every glimpse that I could get, and had to stop myself on more than one occasion from wondering what I might see under the fine clothes he wore.

Every touch made me feel like he was lighting a candle inside my body, and I loved it.

Between the heat of the fire and the small jumps that were part of the dance's basic steps, I could see sweat beginning to bead on Avery's forehead and neck, but still he smiled. I could even see the outline of the binder he wore when he turned. That extra layer had to be roasting him.

I was sure that anyone behind me could see the sweat on the back of my neck, but for once, it didn't bother me. Not with Avery staring at me like I lit up the world. I wasn't sure that I had ever found him more attractive than I did at that moment. I felt as light as air as he led me around the dance floor. If there were a way to bottle this feeling, I would have been a rich woman.

"I wish you didn't have to go back to work," he whispered when he whirled me in a circle. "I know it's really important for you, but I don't want to stop dancing with you."

My heart ached in the best way possible.

"The feeling is mutual, my darling."

The pet name slipped out of my mouth before I could stop it. The other couples, who had not been talking, were now staring at the two of us.

"I plan to fill your dance card at the next ball," he informed me. The twinkle in his eye left me a little breathless.

"I would be delighted to have you fill my dance card," I laughed. "The nobles will talk, though."

"I couldn't give less of a damn about what the other nobles have to say. I don't want this dance to end."

The band moved into the chaconne's coda, signaling that it was time for us to separate and go back into the rows we had begun in.

This time, Avery was the first to pull his arm away. I felt my face fall just a little bit, but I planted the smile back on my face. I gazed across the aisle at the Duke with the goofy grin on his face and knew I had it bad.

AVERY

As the music wound down around me, I found myself struggling to breathe and cursing myself for wearing my binder under my dress coat. I'd wanted to save my energy for the dancing and socializing, rather than spending it all before the evening even started. The spell that allowed my chest to look the way I wanted it to without external forces was an intense one that took a lot of strength.

However, I knew I couldn't blame the binder for all of my breathlessness. I was fairly certain there was no spell in the world that could make me feel as starry eyed as I did right now, staring at Genevieve.

"I should go back to my work," Genevieve whispered.

I simply squeezed her hand and let her go, instantly regretting the loss of contact. She sauntered away from me, and I wasn't sure if the sway in her hips was intentional or not, but it did not go unappreciated.

"Avery, darling! Come here!"

My mother's voice rang out across the ballroom, and I waved. A waiter passed by with a tray of champagne flutes, offering them to the groups of dancers. Grabbing a glass, I made my way to where my parents sat near the ballroom's large stained glass window. I wasn't sure it was actually safe to have this many people packed into the room, but when had Bayard let that get in the way of a good party?

The sun had long since gone down, but as I got closer, I could see the lights from the lanterns that spread out throughout the manicured hedge garden through the colorful, many-paned window.

Father wore a traditional black suit with simple gold ribbing that suited him. If I could see his lapel, I knew I would see the bit of gold embroidery in the Wolvington crest that would match my own. It was well fitted and attractive without being ostentatious, just the way he liked it, with his black hair pulled back from his face with a simple golden circlet that marked his status as the King Father.

Beside him, Mother wore a teal gown with a corset that emphasized her thin waist and broad shoulders before billowing into a wide skirt. She looked beautiful. A long, thin gold chain held a delicately carved Wolvington family crest just above the neckline of her bodice, making it clear to everyone who she was. Her hair was braided into an intricate updo that almost looked like a crown. Father's hand rested gently on one of her shoulders, like always. They were almost always touching when they were together.

It was the perfect party outfit for the serious old man and his fun-loving wife. The glint in their eyes, however, were anything but serious.

Mother peered at me over the half lens of her glasses, one eyebrow cocked and a crooked smile on her face. I knew that look - that meant trouble.

"You were dancing awfully close with that girl, my boy. You are going to cause the whole court to talk about what is going on with you. I presume that was our Ser Genevieve?"

"Yes, Mother," I laughed and tugged at my collar. "May I sit with you? I'm a little overwhelmed after the dancing."

"Let the boy sit, Celeste," Father admonished her with a smile. "You can get all your dirty details while he's comfortable."

She nodded at me, patting the plush chair beside her at the

table. I sat with relief, untying the bottom row of the binder so that I could breathe more easily.

"We weren't dancing that closely, were we?"

Mother's almost black eyes glittered with amusement.

"No, not too closely. But I know you. You are always making sure to be at the height of decorum when it comes to your feminine friends, to avoid gossip."

She leaned forward, placing her elbows on her knees and her chin in her hands.

"You were not worried about decorum when you were dancing with her. You weren't worrying about a thing. There's romance on your mind, my boy. I can see it."

Heat spread to the tips of my ears. She was speaking so loudly! I was sure that the entire ballroom had heard her.

I hadn't been this embarrassed since I'd drunk too much and vomited all over Queen Ines's brand new dancing slippers. And I hadn't even done anything but dance with a beautiful girl this time!

"Mama, don't talk so loud," I muttered. "Look, Julian's coming over! You can bother him about how much he's enjoying his first ball!"

She wagged a finger at me.

"This isn't over, Avery. You forget, we're all going home to the same place tonight and spending the rest of the season together as a family."

"Of course, Mama. I'll tell you all about it when we're home, in private."

She nodded and turned to my nephew with open arms. I knew she wouldn't forget.

CORMAC

The evening had flown by. While there had been a lot of work to do to get the shop back into its usual tidy state after the frenzy of the last few months, the five of us had made easy work of it together. I surveyed the store with tired but proud eyes.

"You go ahead and head home," Poppy told the three apprentices. They didn't hesitate to grab their things and go, chattering about their plans for the rest of the evening.

I had no idea what time it was. The streets around the shop had cleared hours before when the sun went down. Meeting Poppy's eyes from across the shop, I realized that I didn't care. As long as I was with Poppy, I didn't care. The past weeks had been like living in a dream. We had been spending nearly every night together, either in their apartment or mine.

"Would you like me to stay tonight?" I asked, crossing the room in a few long strides and wrapping their small form in my arms. I could feel their heart fluttering where our skin touched. I didn't want to let them go.

"I would like you to stay forever," they murmured.

I was stunned, sure that I hadn't heard them right, but their expression didn't change from the hopeful smile. I took a step back and ran a hand through my hair.

"I'm sorry, can you say that again?"

They were suddenly shy, fiddling with the drawstring on the trousers they had changed into to clean the shop. I stuffed my hands into my pockets to avoid doing the same thing while I waited for them to speak again.

"I said... I want you to stay forever. What would you say if I asked you to move in with me?"

I stared down at them for a moment, taking in the hope that was written all over their face. Their warm eyes were wide under raised brows and they were leaning toward me ever so slightly.

Something fluttered in my chest and I knew my answer without thinking for even a moment longer.

"Of course I'll move in with you..." I looked around the shop thoughtfully, chewing my lip as I smiled back down at them.

"Is there a but?" their voice trembled. "I'm sensing more to that sentence."

"I think we're gonna need someplace a little larger. I don't really want to live somewhere I have to duck under the doorways. But I want to live with you for as long as you'll have me."

Poppy laughed, wrapping their arms around me and snuggling their head into my chest.

"I think we can manage that. We'll start looking for someplace new tomorrow. But for tonight, let's go to bed."

It was like they had read my mind. Taking me by the hand, they led me up the stairs.

GENEVIEVE

The music had wound down, and the guests had long since returned to their respective rooms, or that of a chosen partner, the prince among them. The guard had fulfilled their duty, and I was glad to have rid myself of my sword and pauldrons. After tucking them away in the barracks, I had pulled out a lantern and a knit shawl that Papa had gotten me the prior midwinter, and marched out to the gardens.

It was frigid outside, but there was nothing better than the feeling of the breeze against my skin after the stifling heat and rest of people in the ballroom. To be able to sit instead of stand was also a blessing. The glow of the lantern and the mazelike shrubs around me made me feel like I was the only one in the world, even though I knew that was ridiculous. Closing my eyes, I let myself get lost in the sound and feeling of the wind.

A rustle that had nothing to do with the wind pulled me out of my reverie. My eyes snapped open and without hesitation, I reached for the dagger I always kept in my left boot.

"Who's there?" I called, grateful that my voice didn't waver. I rose from my seat when I didn't get a reply, preparing for a fight if needed, only to see the outline of a familiar and welcome form come around the corner of the hedge maze.

"Avery! What are you doing here?

Thinking fast, I tried to hide the dagger behind my back, but his wide eyes tracked the way that the light glinted of the blade.

"Sorry, I didn't mean to scare you," he said, holding his hands up in a surrender motion. "Were you going to stab me, Genevieve?"

"Only if I needed to," I muttered. "What are you doing out here? Nobody usually makes it this far into the maze."

"I went by the barracks to see if you might want some company that didn't require you to be on watch, and Ser Allondra told me I might find you out here."

Of course she had, I thought, torn between the urge to scowl at my mentor's insistent interference and the excitement that Avery had once again sought out my company. The grin won out.

"I'm impressed you actually found me. It took Alys years to figure out how to find this spot."

He grinned back at me.

"We both know Alys isn't any good at puzzles. I'm surprised she took the time to figure out how to get back here, rather than just blasting her way through the hedges."

I snorted at the idea, and imagining the Queen's face if Alys had done such a thing.

"I think Queen Ines might have had her head for it if she tried. She adores these gardens more than most of her own family."

"To be fair, I've met most of the queen's family, and they're patently terrible," Avery pointed out.

We both burst into giggles, laughing until our stomachs hurt.

"I wasn't going to be the first one to say it."

I sat on the bench, finally stowing the blade back in my boot sheath. Avery moved to join me, but hesitated.

"Mind if I join you?"

I smiled up at him, loving the way the lantern light flickered across his handsome face in the dark. I patted the space on the stone bench next to me. When he didn't move, I realized that he couldn't see the motion in the poorly lit garden.

"Of course, Avery. It would be my pleasure."

My voice was soft, as was the way the light glanced off his smile. His tailcoat swished as he adjusted it to sit beside me. He spread his legs as he made himself comfortable, and didn't pull away when his knee pressed gently against my thigh, though I thought I heard his breath catch in his throat.

I was fairly certain that I'd never been this infatuated with anyone in my life. After the evening we had spent together and the way he was behaving now, I couldn't help but wonder if maybe, just maybe he felt the same way.

"You know, you never answered my question."

"I didn't? What did you ask me?"

"I asked why you made your way out here in the dark to come talk to me."

"I just wanted to spend time with you?" The nervous tremor in his voice made the statement a question. "I wanted to hear how your time being a part of the illustrious honor guard was."

"You'd know just about as well as I do," I laughed, rolling my eyes at him affectionately. "You were watching me just about the whole time, much to Lady Ariana's displeasure."

The smirk on his face was evident in his voice when he

replied. "I see I wasn't the only one paying attention to someone else tonight."

I felt the of a blush creep across my cheeks, silently cursing myself for admitting I'd been watching him all evening instead of his nephew.

"Really, though. I wanted to talk to you and spend some time together, since you were on duty tonight. I know being on the honor guard is a huge honor, despite how boring it actually is."

A small giggle burst from my chest, though I wished I could swallow it.

Avery looked at me with concern, but I flapped a hand at him.

"Sorry, that's just... That's really sweet. I actually enjoyed being on the honor guard, even if my dress did scandalize half the noblemen at court.

"It's far too easy to scandalize them. My mother liked your dress, by the way. She intends to quiz me all about you and our relationship once I get home."

"Oh? And what will you tell her?"

I answered coyly, as if I didn't care what his answer was. In reality, my insides were roiling at the thought of what he might tell his mother about me and what that meant for our relationship.

Our thighs were still touching on the bench when I felt his body shift so that he was facing me straight on.

His lips were slightly parted as he looked into my eyes. My heart began to race. His hand brushed mine sending shivers up my spine.

"I know that your sister originally reached out to me because your mother was badgering you about getting into a relationship, and that you had always had a crush on me," he started slowly, gaining confidence as he spoke. "I wondered... if perhaps those feelings were still there for you now that you actually know me? Because I've come to care quite deeply about you in these last weeks, and I think-"

"Avery."

I cut him off, squeezing his thigh. He nearly leaped from the bench, his face suddenly stricken. The words tumbled from his lips.

"Oh, god. I'm so sorry. I got the wrong impression and if I was too forward-"

I grabbed both of his soft hands and pulled myself up so that I was standing. I could see that his chin trembled slightly, a total change from the hope that had shone in it just moments before.

"That wasn't what I was trying to say at all!" I burst out, cutting him off again. "I was just trying to tell you we weren't alone and that we need to find somewhere else to talk if we want privacy, which I do."

"What?" His face puckered in confusion.

"There are two people in the hedges behind us rather passionately enjoying the dark solitude of the garden together. Can't you hear them?"

As the realization dawned on him that I wasn't rejecting him, his face bloomed like a flower. We heard a throaty groan followed by a high pitched gasp. I resisted the urge to giggle like a schoolgirl at the situation.

Then something dawned on me. I knew exactly where to take him.

"Come on, I know just the place to get away from everyone."

Keeping his hands tightly in my own, I led him away from the bench to a place where I knew we wouldn't be interrupted.

AVERY

My heart felt like it had been out at sea during a hurricane or ridden an entirely unbroken horse at a full gallop - tossed about and thoroughly beaten.

Of all the things I had expected to happen when I poured out my feelings to a girl I thought I might love, being interrupted by an amorous couple in a hedge was not one of them.

It had taken me nearly half an hour after the ball to get the courage to even go talk to Genevieve, let alone convince myself that it would be all right for me to interrupt her in the hedge maze. My stomach heaved at the thought of spilling my guts to her all over again, but I couldn't stand the idea of ending the night without knowing if I had a chance.

She still held one of my hands in hers, leading me on a twisting path that I would never be able to recreate on my own - even in the daylight.

"How do you know your way through this maze so well?" I asked, slightly breathless at the pace she was setting. It was hard to take a deep breath, thanks to the binder I still wore, along with my nervousness and the cold night air. "Can we slow down a little?"

"Oh, I'm sorry!" she slowed to a halt and set the lamp on the ground. The light that it let off was almost spooky. "I forget that not everybody is quite as in shape as I am. Are you okay to keep going? We're almost where I wanted to take you."

"Just... Give me a minute to catch my breath, and I'll be all right. I don't know how you are moving as fast as you are with all that chainmail on."

If it was this difficult for me to breathe in a binder, I couldn't imagine what it would feel like to be wearing what was essentially a metal corset in the frigid air. She released my hand and grinned at me.

"A whole lot of practice. Plus, it's cold. Movement gets the blood pumping."

"I see."

I didn't, really. I much preferred to curl up in front of a blazing fire with a good story, though I could see the merits of her thought process. We fell into silence while I tried to get my breathing under control.

Once I was ready to move again, I reached out my hand to her again. She took it in hers. Goosebumps that had nothing to do with the weather outside spread across my skin as we began walking. There was a purposefulness to her stride that I couldn't help but admire.

Turning a carefully trimmed corner into an open clearing, the air around us became just a bit crisper. Glancing around, I tried to discern where exactly we were in the palace gardens, but it was too dark to see anything. Genevieve's hand released mine and I felt the loss like that of a limb. The world around me went dark.

I turned to look for her but couldn't find her in the darkness. A giggle interrupted my search, and I whirled towards it.

I couldn't see anything in the darkness, not even the light she had carried.

"Where is here, exactly?"

"Take three steps forward and one step to the left and you'll find me. Your eyes will adjust to the darkness soon enough. Trust me."

Sure enough, she was right. As my eyes adjusted, I started walking, holding my hands out in front of me, hoping to avoid running into anything I couldn't see. When my hands brushed against metal, I knew I'd gone too far. The only thing at chest height that would be metal would be... the...

"Well, if you just wanted to cop a feel, we could have just stayed in the hedge maze!" Genevieve laughed.

I blushed furiously, stammering an apology and curling my hands away from her. She grabbed them before I could get them into my pockets, tugging me closer with a smile.

"Now, we were talking about feelings, were we not? I think we can continue this discussion once the lights are on." She let go of one hand and carefully lit two tall lamps that I hadn't even seen behind her.

"That's much better, don't you think?"

I knew the blush was still clear on my cheeks, and she could see it now that the area around us was lit. Not trusting actual words to come out of my mouth at that moment, I nodded. Luckily, Genevieve wasn't one to waste time when she knew her mind.

"You asked me if the crush I had on you was still here. Well, it isn't."

Her words were like a blow to the chest. Why had she brought me out here if she was just going to tell me exactly what I thought she was saying in the garden?

"My feelings for you have turned into something completely different since I've started to actually get to know you. My crush on you was based entirely on someone I'd built up in my head."

I opened my mouth to speak but she held up a finger.

"The real you is a million times better. Every second that we have spent together has been better than the one before, and I don't want our time to end."

I nearly fell over from the impact of what she'd said. She liked me. She liked the real me. And I liked her, too. I took a step closer to her, biting my bottom lip.

"Genevieve... I would really like to kiss you right now."

My voice was breathy and rough, and I didn't even care.

"How convenient," she replied, taking a step closer. "I would very much like to be kissed."

The cold breeze brought a sweet floral scent with a metal undertone that I instantly knew was Genevieve's scent. I reached out a hand and she placed hers in my palm. With a gentle tug, she wrapped her other arm around my waist. Her touch was intoxicating. Desire pooled in my stomach, intense and warm.

My gaze darted to her lips and back to her eyes, making sure this was what she wanted. Her eyes were focused on the movement of my tongue over my lips. I pressed my lips to hers and the whole world dropped away when she responded instantly, hungrily. Our mouths moved together and when she nibbled on my bottom lip, my knees nearly went out from under me.

Kissing wasn't new to me. I'd kissed plenty of women in my time, but kissing them had never felt anywhere near as perfect as kissing Genevieve. I never wanted to stop kissing her.

She broke away, breathing raggedly, and pressed her forehead to mine. My lips were buzzing.

"Avery... We have to stop. People will see us. Our reputations..."

I laughed lightly, trailing my hand down her cheek. She shivered, pressing her face into my palm.

"I don't give a damn about our reputations," I told her. "This court could use a scandal with some truth to it, don't you think?"

She smiled and pressed a soft kiss to my palm before pulling away. I felt the loss of contact like the loss of a limb, but I let her go. She was right of course. If we kept at it like this, we would soon find ourselves pressed up against the brick wall with my hand up her skirt.

When there was some space between us, she spoke again.

"How about we take this to the next step?"

I was confused.

"What do you consider the next step?"

"Well, you've met my family, and I've met your mother, but that is hardly the same. We need to have dinner with your family. As a pair."

"I will make all the arrangements for as soon as possible. Just the two of us and my parents. I suspect it will be at least a week before we can make a date of it, though."

She smiled at me in the lamplight and I feared I might swoon. How embarrassing that would be.

"Then I shall await your letter that it is settled. Until then, there shall be no more canoodling in gardens."

I laughed aloud at that.

"In that case, may I at least escort you back to the barracks, my lady?"

"It would be my pleasure."

1 0

I swiped the back of my hand across my forehead and groaned when it came away sticky with sweat. I could not believe how disgustingly hot it was in here, though it didn't really surprise me because I couldn't see to the front of the door for all the people in the shop. We hadn't been this busy in all the years I'd been in business, and it had been like this ever since the ball had ended.

I spied at least three other knights in the shop, waiting patiently to talk to Isabela about what their order would be, but I suspected that our knit chainmail would be very popular in the coming season.

Thanks to the two gowns I'd made for the Teagan ladies, and the huge splash Genevieve's gown had made with the other knights, I suspected that my assistants and I would have enough work to more than pay for the new, taller home that Cormac and I had decided to purchase on the outskirts of the Crafter's district. It would make it much more pleasant for both of us to be able to work on a project together when we didn't have to lug a bunch of tools outside of our at-home workshops.

Thanks to more than a week of steady business, Isabela and I had worked out a system. She would sort them into categories - clothes that she and Maria could handle, and clothes that I would have to create a pattern for on my own for them to help with. If we kept at this rate, I'd probably need to hire another assistant or put Isabela on as a full time seamstress. She was nearly ready for it.

But I had no more time for musing. I could see Isabela pointing an older woman with eyebrows so thick they nearly reached her receding hairline without effort. I didn't recognize her, so she must have something difficult for me to work on.

Wonderful, I thought as I cracked my fingers and pasted my customer service smile back onto my face. Time to get to work.

GENEVIEVE

I couldn't remember the last time I'd been this anxious. Maybe right before I was knighted, but never before a dinner. I couldn't stop pacing the room even though there were hours before I needed to even start getting dressed.

While there were a few reasons I was nervous, I knew they were all ridiculous. No, the King wouldn't rescind my knighthood. Avery wouldn't suddenly decide he hated me. It was very unlikely that the family would lose all of its land in one night. And yet, those were the worries that were crossing through my mind as I moved through my room.

It had been two weeks since the ball and it was the first time I would officially be meeting Avery's family as a romantic partner.

Alys had helped me choose the perfect gown to wear from our shopping trip and I had nothing else to do until it was time to go.

"Well, I might as well put this energy to good use," I declared aloud. There was no one else in the room but it felt more real that way. My weapons hadn't been properly oiled since the ball two weeks prior, as I'd been out of the whale oil that I needed to care for them properly. Focusing on fixing that would take my mind off of the dinner ahead of me.

Striding across the room, I flung open the doors to the mahogany wardrobe that held my personal cache of weaponry. I took a deep breath, letting the comforting, lightly tangy scent of iron and steel wash over me before grasping the wrapped leather handles of my short swords and pulling them off of the rack. The weight of my favorite weapons in my arms was relaxing.

I turned towards the table that sat opposite the wardrobe and sighed. It was covered in papers. Unless I wanted to render all of the papers unusable afterwards, I needed to clean it first.

I hadn't realized just how slovenly I'd become in the weeks leading up to the ball. If Ser Allondra saw this, I'd be cleaning latrines for a week. If my mother saw it... I didn't even want to think about what she'd do. I knew better than to leave my space in this kind of disarray.

I put the swords back where they belonged and plopped myself gracelessly into the upholstered chair that had been a gift from my grandmother to begin sorting. I had a time honored system for dealing with my paperwork - sorting them into piles.

The personal letters I sorted into two piles of their own - answered and unanswered. Some of the answered ones would be turning into fire starters later. Others, I intended to keep and scrape down for reuse. Vellum was pricey, even for us. Household paperwork got its own pile and notes to myself got another.

Within a quarter of an hour, there was enough space on the table for me to lay out and clean my blades. I retrieved the small glass bottle of oil and two cloths from my travel bag. I wiggled the stopper of the bottle open. The fishy scent of the thin oil filled the room. Anyone not used to the smell would have called it pungent, but it was as familiar to me as the scent of my mother's cologne.

Lowering myself back into the chair, I tilted the bottle so it would coat the well-used polishing cloth in my other hand, stopping when it was moist enough to work but not dripping. There was no point in wasting the expensive oil.

Placing the bottle on the table and stoppering it for safekeeping, I picked up one of the swords. The blades were sturdy, without much in the way of decoration, but I loved them. Most of my time training for my knighthood was spent practicing with weapons I could use on horseback - a lance, a bow and arrow, or a sword and shield. I knew why, but I had always had a preference for close combat. These swords allowed me to surprise my opponents with my speed, and kept them too busy to use their often heavier weight and height advantage against me on the battlefield.

Muscle memory took over as I worked, rubbing the oil down the length of the blade over and over again. I took extra care of the peening block that connected the base of the blade to the hilt, buffing away even the hint of rust or damage.

I lost track of time as I worked, switching from blade to blade without stopping. With each stroke, my thoughts got quieter and calmer, until a knock startled me into nearly dropping the dagger in my hand.

A moment later, the door opened and Juniper poked their head in. They didn't look surprised to see me working my way through my personal armory, though they did wrinkle their button nose at the smell.

"I wondered what that smell was. Miss, you have about three hours until dinner, and I thought you might want to bathe. Unless you want to show up at the palace smelling like the wharfs."

I grimaced, realizing they had a point. Duchess Celeste and King Father Victor would be less than thrilled if someone hoping to join their family showed up smelling the way I surely did right now.

Juniper laughed and gestured at the table in front of me.

"I'll have water heated for you in a jiffy. Tidy up and we'll have you smelling like a person again soon."

"Thank you, Juniper. You're the best."

They grinned at me and dipped a curtsy.

"I know, Miss."

Before I knew it, the door was closing behind me. I shook my head, smiling. Juniper was one of the best servants I'd ever hired and I was glad that they knew it. Now I just had to make sure that I looked -and smelled- my best for the evening ahead.

AVERY

I couldn't keep myself from bouncing on my toes as I waited outside the main hall of the palace for Genevieve's carriage to arrive. She was due to be here any moment for our first ever family dinner, and I couldn't wait to introduce her to Father.

Mother was, of course, thrilled to have her. Apparently they had hit it off quite well while they shopped. Mother had told Father that he would have absolutely no reason to object to a union between us, which had set us all at ease. Father was an excellent judge of character, but he tended to be a little harsher than necessary when it came to new people. It came from a lifetime of strategizing to keep his crown and family safe, something I couldn't blame him for. I so wanted him to love Genevieve as much as I did.

Before my nerves could get the better of me, a carriage built out of dark wood pulled up, led by two beautiful black geldings. My heart fluttered when I saw the carved seal of House Teagan on the side.

A footman I didn't recognize opened the door and a slippered foot stepped out. My breath caught in my throat as the rest of Genevieve's body followed it.

Her dress was a silvery lilac confection, fitted tight around her torso and blooming into a skirt that billowed out around her legs. She got more stunning every time that I saw her, something I hoped would never go away, no matter how long we were together.

When she set foot on the ground, I bowed.

"Welcome to the palace, lady knight. May I say, you are looking particularly lovely tonight?"

Her cheeks flushed a pale pink that made my heart skip and my smile widen. With a deep curtsy, she replied, "You may, my lord duke. You are looking quite handsome yourself."

Holding out my arm to her, I grinned.

"May I escort you to dinner, Genevieve? There are two people there who are very excited to spend time with you."

She blinked rapidly, rubbing at the skin of her wrists before she noticed my attention. She was nervous. I noticed she was wearing a silver cuff with a floral design on it that complemented the sheen of her gown. She dropped her hands to her sides and cleared her throat. Her smile only trembled slightly as I took both of her callused hands in mine.

"They're going to love you," I whispered. "Just like I do."

She blinked her hazel eyes at me rapidly.

"Are you sure?"

"Positive. Mother has been singing your praises all week and Father trusts her judgement implicitly."

Her cheeks colored slightly deeper. I couldn't have taken my eyes off of her even if I wanted to. And I didn't. Taking a deep breath, she met my gaze and smiled for real this time.

"Then it would be my honor to come to dinner with you, Avery."

———

GENEVIEVE

Nervous as I was, I had to admit that walking into the palace dining room on Avery's arm felt wonderful. I had not realized just how good it would feel, to be dressed in a beautiful gown and on the arm of a wonderful man that I was already falling hard for. I had been trained to fall properly, so I wouldn't get hurt, but I knew full well that my training would be absolutely useless.

The dining room was magnificent, the walls draped in rich velvet and beautiful landscapes painted in oil. The table was set with beautiful china and a large bowl filled with oranges and berries of all sorts. I noticed that there were far too many place settings at the table for the dinner I'd expected.

A tall, thin man who looked as if he had been born in the palace's starched uniform bowed to us both forcing me to stop perusing the room around us.

"What would you like to drink, Your Grace? We have tea, lemonade and a delicious madeira wine that would suit this evening's fish course nicely."

I couldn't tell if the question was directed at Avery or myself, but Avery took the lead.

"A glass of wine sounds perfect, thank you, Claude. What would you care for, Genevieve?"

"The wine sounds delightful, thank you, but could I also ask for a glass of water? I don't want to risk overindulging."

"Of course, Your Grace."

With another bow, he left us to our own devices and I turned to Avery, feeling a frown crease my forehead. Had he known we were having more guests?

"Avery, that table is set for eight. Who else is joining us?"

His gaze roved the table and his mouth formed into an "oh." Before he could answer, the double doors behind the table were flung open, revealing King Bayard and Queen Ines, followed by the King Father Victor and Duchess Celeste, and then the prince and princess. Without a moment's hesitation, I dropped into the deepest curtsy possible, my knees nearly touching the ground and the crown of my head pointing at the royal family.

The protocol was the only thing keeping me from hyperventilating at that moment. This was not at all what I had expected. I had never been this close to the entire royal family in my life. I'd hardly even been in the King's presence except for my knighting ceremony, and even then, it had been for a mere quarter of an hour.

"Please rise, dear girl," Queen Ines's sweet voice rang out. I held my pose for a few racing heartbeats longer before I rose, keeping my eyes on the floor. She laughed lightly. "You are practically family at this point. That's what we're here to celebrate."

"I - Your Highness?"

I rocked back on my heels. My voice was several octaves higher than usual and I hated it. I sounded like a silly school girl. Beside me, Avery was standing with his mouth agape. With a shake of his head, he turned to me and placed his mouth near my ear.

"Genevieve, I'm so sorry. I had no idea. Are you all right?"

"Please pardon me, your Highnesses. I need to use the restroom." Without waiting for a response from everyone who outranked me, I fled from the room.

AVERY

I watched as Genevieve ran from the room, her skirts held up so she could stride as if she were wearing trousers. As soon as she was gone, I whirled on my family, my cheeks aflame with anger.

"What in the Goddess's name were you thinking, springing that on us? It was just supposed to be Mother and Father. I was going to ease her into the whole 'part of the royal family' thing," I roared. They all stared at me for a moment, then Bayard snorted, drawing everyone's attention.

"She's a knight, I would have thought she'd be braver than that."

Ines swatted him, a frown on her painted pink lips.

"You didn't tell me that she wasn't aware we were coming to dinner, Bayard."

"In my defense, I didn't tell you that *we* were coming to dinner until an hour ago."

"That isn't a defense, my boy," Father growled. "Really, you ought to take more care with your schedule."

I rolled my eyes, trying to keep my temper in check. This was an entirely typical family argument, but it shouldn't have been happening.

"That doesn't change the fact that *no one told me* and I couldn't tell her, and now she's hiding in the restroom."

My mother's eyes were the only ones focused on me now.

"Go after her, Avery. Apologize to her for me and bring her back when she's ready. Everyone will be nice, I promise."

That last bit was in a tone that I was familiar with from childhood. My mother would allow nothing else. Nodding at her, I ran after Genevieve, guessing at where she had turned.

There were all number of places she could have gone. The palace was full of all kinds of passageways and easy places to hide, especially in the royal wing. Hopefully, one of the servants would have actually pointed her to the nearest bathroom. After asking several, I found one who had seen her.

Instead of sending her to the restroom, however, one of the maids had pointed her to my chambers. Why she had done that, I had no idea, but at least it would make it easier to find her. When I reached the door, I paused. I couldn't hear anything through the thick door, but that wasn't surprising. The rooms were designed to be nearly soundproof. I rapped my knuckles against the door three times and waited. After what felt like an eternity, I heard the shuffle of slippered footsteps and then the door opened.

She had gone pale and her eyes were red, as if she'd been crying.

"Oh, Genevieve, I'm so sorry. I had no idea - Mother didn't mention and my brother is... well, he's a pain in the ass."

She yelped, eyes widening at my words.

"You cannot call the King a pain in the ass in his own palace, Avery!"

I shot her a wicked smile that seemed to calm her somewhat.

"I didn't call the *king* a pain in the ass. I called my *brother* a pain in the ass. It's different."

"It is not," she groaned and opened the door wide enough that I could actually walk into my own room without running into her. "If you insist on talking like this, will you commit treason in private, not in the public of the hallway?"

"Gladly."

It was warm in the room. I guessed whoever had shown Genevieve to the room had stoked the fire, as I distinctly remembered banking the coals before I'd left for the main hall.

"May I say something?"

She sighed, waving a hand at me.

"You may, but if you come out with any more surprises, I may flee the palace entirely."

I nodded, knowing my face was as serious as I felt.

"Genevieve, since meeting you, you have become the light of my days, and I soon suspect you will become the love of my life." She gasped but I continued. "I know that my family can be a lot to handle, which is why I was hoping to ease you into it, but they are going to love you nearly as much as I do. I promise to protect you from anything they can throw at you, physical or verbal."

She looked like she was on the verge of tears.

"Can... can I have a few minutes to collect myself?"

I nodded, wrapping my arms around her until I could hear her heartbeat fluttering against my chest. She laid her head against my shoulder and took a deep breath.

"We can stay here for as long as you like. They will wait."

GENEVIEVE

By the time we re-entered the room half an hour later, I felt much more at ease. Avery's hand was wrapped tightly around mine, the way it had been ever since we left his chambers. Even looking into the faces of the entire royal family, all three generations, I thought I could handle this. I gulped as Claude announced us to the room, and plastered on a smile that hid all of my misgivings.

Those royal faces in varying shades of brown from the lightest of balsa wood to rich teak all smiled back at me with what looked like genuine affection. I glanced at Avery and saw the truth of his love for me in his eyes. I could do this. *We* could do this.

Together, I was fairly certain we could take on any enemy in the world and be just fine. And that included his parents. King Father Victor rose from the table and gave me a slight bow, which surprised me.

"I would like to apologize for my family, Ser Genevieve. We did not mean to surprise you with extra company. This dinner came together at the last minute for my eldest son and his family. If you'd like, I will happily send them away,"

That shocked me. I glanced at Avery again and saw that he was as surprised as I was. But I didn't want him to send them away. Not yet, anyway.

"That won't be necessary, Your Highness. I look forward to spending time with your entire family." I took a deep breath. "What is on the menu tonight?"

King Bayard began to answer, but Claude stepped up with an artfully decorated menu. It was to be a four course meal with a mushroom salad, white soup, a tuna pie with soy, ginger and shallots, and a raspberry trifle for dinner. They were going all out. Avery squeezed my hand, and I knew it was all going to be okay, as long as we were together.

CORMAC

I let my gaze travel around the apartment I'd been living in for the last fifteen years. Everything I owned had been packed into crates and baskets. Despite the fact that the walls had been cleared of everything and washed down, the room didn't feel empty. Just like my heart, it was full of all of the memories I'd made here. It hardly felt real.

I'd cooked my first meal in the city in this kitchenette, hosted several different apprentices and learned more about myself in this room and this forge than I had in the first forty years of my life.

Everything was changing, and I couldn't wait to start the next chapter of my life with Poppy as equal partners, my heart safe in their hands.

ACKNOWLEDGMENTS

I have a lot of people to thank for helping to make this book happen.

To Chris, for making dinner on nights when I couldn't drag myself away from the computer and listening to me whine about everything my characters were doing without permission. You are the light of my life and I look forward to sharing all the rest of my days with you.

To my mom, who swore she'd still love me even if I had six eyeballs, which I promptly put to the test by dying my hair bright blue.

To my sister, who answered a lot of really ridiculous questions for me as I was writing this.

To Amara, Abigail, Lina and X for all of their cheering and support while I worked my way through the many iterations of this novel.

Last, but never least, to all of my readers. You all are the reason I'm able to do this, and I am so blessed to have every single one of you. Thank you for reading my stories and telling other people about them. I honestly never believed anyone but my close friends would buy these books, and I am delighted to be wrong with each book I sell.

ABOUT THE AUTHOR

Ceillie Simkiss is a queer and neurodivergent author and freelance writer based in southern Virginia. She has bylines in the Danville Register & Bee, VIDA Magazine, Culturess and Global Comment. She blogs regularly on her website, CandidCeillie.com and is the owner and editor of LetsFoxAboutIt.com.

She loves nothing more than curling up in bed with a book and her many furry creatures, but playing silly video games is a close second, even though she's terrible at them. She also writes as Candace Harper.

It is easiest to reach her on Twitter or via email! She would love to hear from you!

facebook.com/ceilliesimkiss

twitter.com/candidceillie

instagram.com/candidceillie

goodreads.com/18190082.Ceillie_Simkiss

bookbub.com/authors/ceillie-simkiss